TAKEN BY MAGIC

THE BAINE CHRONICLES: BOOK 8

JASMINE WALT

DYNAMO PRESS

Cover illustration by Judah Dobin. Cover typography by Rebecca Frank. Edited by Mary Burnett.

❀ Created with Vellum

1

"I can't believe we have a party scheduled every other day this month," I groused as our carriage rumbled up the winding hillside road leading to Lady Porgillas's mansion. "Don't these people understand we have a state to run?"

Iannis gently dug his thumb into my shoulder, which was knotted with tension. "Such things matter little to our hosts when there is an upcoming wedding," he said as I moaned in relief. "All of our wealthy constituents are trying to one-up each other with these lavish parties and gifts, and as Lady Porgillas donated quite a substantial one, we cannot slight her by ignoring her invitation."

"Nobody asked her to get that fountain," I grumbled, but it was half-hearted. Lady Porgillas had donated a twelve-foot marble fountain sculpture of Magorah—traditionally depicted as a warrior in a wolf pelt—for the newly rebuilt square in Shifter-town. It was a generous gesture, and one I especially could not ignore as a half-shifter myself. The residents of Shiftertown had been thrilled to receive it, and the fact that it had come from a mage went a long way toward improving race relations.

"Why did she have that sculpture created, anyway?" I asked Iannis as the mansion finally came into view. "Does Lady Porgillas have some kind of soft spot for shifters?"

Iannis shrugged. "Not that I have heard. But she knows that you do, and like I said, our wealthier citizens are all trying to one-up each other just now. It was quite a clever gift on her part."

I nodded as the carriage doors opened and a liveried footman helped us to the ground. The skirts of the steel blue gown I'd chosen for the evening rustled a little as I alighted, and I quickly checked to make sure it hadn't snagged on anything. The first time I'd attended one of these gatherings, I'd somehow managed to get the end of my skirt jammed in a door closing behind me, and the fabric had ripped before I'd realized what had happened. An easy fix, now that I had Fenris's vast magical knowledge at my disposal, but there had been quite a few people around to witness the blunder, and the last thing I needed was to walk into this hoity-toity mansion with a rip in my skirt.

The thought of Fenris sent a pang of sadness through me, and I forced myself to push it aside. He was alive, I knew, and there was no point in dwelling on his absence. He would contact us when he was ready to be found again.

If *he's ever ready to be found again.*

Lady Porgillas's mansion was tall and imposing and surrounded by park-like gardens, as favored by wealthy mages. Since it was an hour from the city, she could have as much space as she wanted. I was getting to know this lifestyle quite well, with all these parties I was attending. I supposed I should count myself lucky that we'd rejected a good portion of the invitations— otherwise we'd be attending two to three parties per *night*, which would have driven me up a wall.

Pushing that unpleasant thought out of my mind, I took an appreciative sniff of the fresh evening air, cleaner than in the city —the linden trees lining the drive were in bloom, almost over-powering in the early summer air. The sun was just setting over the sea, but there wasn't much time for me to admire our surroundings. Iannis took my arm, and I curled my fingers around his forearm as he led me up the steps and into the mansion. Iannis had our invitation, but the guard at the entrance waved us through without even asking to see it— nobody ever failed to recognize the Chief Mage and his shifter bride, not after our names and faces had been plastered across every newspaper in the Federation. Besides, we were supposed to be the guests of honor tonight.

"Lord Iannis!" Lady Porgillas greeted us with a warm smile as we entered the packed ballroom. She was a slim redhead who wore her three hundred and fifty years lightly. "Welcome to my little party. Everyone is agog to meet you."

A sea of robes and dresses filled the gigantic space, and as I swept my gaze across the floor, I noted that there were only mages in attendance.

"And the lovely Miss Baine. I am so pleased you could make it."

"Thank you for inviting us," Iannis said, briefly bending over the lady's hand and kissing it.

"And for your generous gift," I added with a smile of my own as I shook our hostess's hand. "The residents of Shiftertown are very pleased."

"I'm delighted to hear that," she said. "I thought a fountain sculpture would be just the thing to liven up that drab little square of theirs." The way she said it, with just the slightest note of condescension in her voice, told me exactly what she thought of Shiftertown and its denizens, and I blinked.

"Have you actually been there, then?" I asked. I had figured she had chosen a depiction of Magorah simply because everyone knew that he was the shifter god, but perhaps she knew more about shifters than she was letting on.

Lady Porgillas shrugged. "Once, to assist with the relief efforts after the quake. I am so lucky that my mansion out here among the vineyards was properly warded...I hear that things are much improved in Solantha since that dreadful day."

"Yes," Iannis cut in smoothly, "and we greatly appreciate all you've done for us." He gave me a subtle warning glance, and I bit back a sigh. I knew I shouldn't feel so defensive about Shiftertown, especially since she had given such a great gift. I just wished it had been out of true generosity rather than a desire to impress her fellow mages, and particularly Iannis.

Still, it was better than a poke in the eye with a sharp stick.

Eventually, Iannis and I moved on to mingle with the rest of the crowd. All of the mages we talked to were almost irritatingly polite to our faces. However, a few hung back, eyeing me with barely concealed disdain, and I left a trail of whispers in my wake that I did my best to tune out. I was well aware that not everyone approved of my match with Iannis, but they could stick their jealousy and condemnation up their asses. The only thing that mattered was our love and commitment for each other, and that was as strong as it had ever been.

Still, when I stopped by the refreshment table to fill a plate with crab cakes, tiny salmon rolls, and goose liver canapés, I couldn't help but overhear a gaggle of women nearby.

"Look at her. That's the third plate she's taken tonight. How is she not bursting out of the seams of her dress?"

"I hear shifters have very high metabolisms and can eat whatever they want." The other mage tittered. *"Even so, that dress is a pretty tight fit."*

"Well, it's understandable that she would not want to wear apprentice robes to an affair like this and remind everyone of her lowly status. One does wonder when the Chief Mage and she find time to practice?"

"He finds time enough to tumble her, I'd bet. Though how he can bring himself to—"

"I know what you mean. Shifters are savages, and she is no different. Just look at those animal eyes of hers. I guess there must be some kind of kinky appeal; there's no accounting for tastes. And yet she prances around with her head high, as though she were as good as any of us."

My fingers tightened on the gold-plated tongs I was holding, and

I had to force myself to let go before I accidentally bent them. Taking a deep breath through my nose, I forced myself to calm down. I'd heard it all before, and would probably continue to hear it no matter how far I got in life. Bigots rarely ever changed their minds—the best way to ensure that their hatred didn't spread was to simply not pay them any attention.

"This absurd match cannot go well. I wonder how long into their marriage until the Chief Mage starts looking for a mistress?"

My resolve to ignore them abruptly snapped. Seeing red, I quickly riffled through my magical repertoire, searching for a suitable spell that could be cast at a distance. I hid a smile when I found the perfect thing, then subtly flicked my hand toward their group and muttered the Words under my breath.

While the magic did its work, I sauntered over to an older mage with my plate of finger food and struck up a conversation. It turned out that he was a weather mage, and as I half-listened to his talk about storms and wind patterns, I looked toward the group of gossips out of the corner of my eye. They were continuing to make snide remarks about me, but unbeknownst to them, something strange was very gradually happening to their clothing.

"By the Lady," one of them exclaimed after a while. "Myrna, you must have washed this set of robes one too many times. I can see straight through them!"

Myrna, who was an older mage with silver hair, gasped as she looked down at herself. I angled my head a little more toward them and saw that Myrna's deep blue robes had become very sheer, exposing a bony frame and mismatched underwear. But the other woman...

"Stacia!" one of the other women gasped. "You aren't wearing any underwear at all!"

"What in Recca is going on?" the weather mage asked, craning his neck to look over my shoulder. I turned around fully, and bit back a laugh—everyone else was now gawking at the five women, whose saggy arms and spindly, unshaven legs were on full display for everyone to see. The most amusing were the two who had used illusion to make their faces appear more youthful, while leaving everything else beneath their robes untouched. I guessed they thought they were saving magic, but they wouldn't make that mistake again.

"Why, this is outrageous!" Myrna made a sharp gesture and quickly muttered a spell. The robes immediately returned to normal, though the mages' expressions did not—all five women were red-faced and in various states of anger and embarrass-ment. "Who did this?" she demanded loudly. "Come forward at once!"

But no one said anything, and as the snickers from the other guests continued to grow, the women began to shrink back in embarrassment. I was tempted to meet Myrna's eyes and give her a big smile, but instead, I looked at Iannis. He was on the far side of the room conversing with a middle-aged woman, but when our eyes met, he gave me a subtle wink.

"Try not to make a habit of it," he suggested as he turned back to

the man he was talking to. *"If clothes begin to disappear at every event we attend, we shan't be invited back again."*

"Then I will make every effort to make sure that it happens," I teased.

I felt his laughter down the mindspeak connection before I severed it, then apologized to the weather mage and gave him my attention again. The rest of the evening wore on, with boring conversation after boring conversation, but the results from my little magical prank were enough to keep a smile on my face. Luckily, most of the mages had a few glasses of wine in them, so it wasn't exactly difficult to pretend to be interested—some of them were drunk enough that they would have carried on a conversation with a wall without noticing.

Eventually we sat down for a six-course dinner featuring lobster bisque, trout soufflé, roast duck, beef with pineapple sauce, oven-fried buttered mangoes, and marzipan pudding, with different and probably very expensive wines for every course. There would be some dancing afterward, and then Iannis and I would finally be able to make our getaway. Maybe we'd even get a bit of alone time for once. Our sex life had taken a nosedive these past few months, with all the rebuilding efforts plus the wedding planning taking most of our attention and time. Only nine more weeks now—I couldn't wait for it all to be over.

When the meal finally came to an end, Lady Porgillas tapped her glass with her fork to get everyone's attention. "Before we begin dancing," she said, "how about we demonstrate some of our latest achievements? I know there are a few of us here tonight who have recently mastered interesting new spells."

The crowd reacted enthusiastically to this suggestion, and I buried a groan. This wasn't the first time I'd been forced to endure a magical "show-and-tell," and it was always embarrassing because as an apprentice with less than two years of training, I couldn't very well perform high-level spells. The last thing I needed was people noticing that I was way ahead of the curriculum. So I was always forced to perform some relatively easy spell, and the mages would titter behind their hands at the "cute little apprentice" who was so out of her league.

"This is stupid," I grumbled to Iannis as the first mage stood up and conjured a flaming bird that soared around the room, showering us with embers. The room gasped when the embers turned into rubies upon hitting the ground. I picked mine up, and it sat in the palm of my hand for a moment before vanishing. I had no doubt the ruby had been real, but manufacturing coins and gemstones without official leave by the Federation was considered illegal, so of course the mage couldn't let us keep them.

"I don't see any reason why you can't show off a little bit," Iannis said, slipping his hand into mine beneath the table. *"After all, we are planning to graduate you early as a 'fast learner.' If you don't demonstrate that you are making above-average progress, it will seem suspicious if we tell them a year from now you are all finished."*

"Really?" I perked right up at that. *"Are you sure it's okay?"*

Iannis smiled. *"I don't see the harm. Fenris is gone anyway—it won't affect his safety if you show these mages some of your accomplishments."*

The mention of Fenris sobered us both, and I squeezed his hand. *"I wish he was here with us,"* I said quietly as we watched another mage perform. *"He was supposed to stand with you on our wedding day."*

"The wedding is still over two moons away," Iannis said. *"We may yet hear from him before then."*

Yes, but that didn't mean Fenris would return to Solantha. And I couldn't blame him. The Federal Director of Security, Garrett Toring, had come dangerously close to figuring out the truth—if I hadn't convinced him that Fenris was Polar ar'Tollis's son, rather than Polar in permanent disguise, he would likely still be on his manhunt right now. Maybe I could convince Fenris to come back if I told him about that cover story, but it was hardly safe to talk about such deadly secrets over the phone.

"I'd like to take a turn," I announced, standing up. Maybe Fenris couldn't be with us, but his memories and knowledge were right here, in my head, and I would honor him tonight by making full use of them.

"Of course, Miss Baine," Lady Porgillas said, gesturing to the makeshift stage that had been set up. "We all would love to see what Lord Iannis has been teaching you."

A murmur rippled through the room, which I ignored as I took the stage. Everybody knew that masters and apprentices weren't supposed to engage in an amorous relationship, and Iannis and I had smashed that rule into the dust. Judging from that gossip earlier, people were wondering if the apprenticeship was just a pretext. Well, I'd show them.

"Lord Iannis and I have been practicing weather magic lately," I announced to the room as I lifted my arms. Several people shifted in their chairs at that, and I gave them a fierce smile as I quietly spoke a complicated spell under my breath. The air in the room stirred to life, a mere breeze at first, but as the magic built, it quickly grew into a raging windstorm. The crowd gasped, ducking down as the chandeliers began to swing wildly. Two curtains were torn down from the windows, and several women shrieked as pins were torn from their hair, their careful coiffures undone by the wild winds. Platters rattled, silverware clattered to the floor, and several wine-glasses were toppled, sending rivers of red down the white tablecloths. A veritable tornado had invaded the elegant dining room. It felt amazing, and from the alarmed expressions around me, I was playing right into the cliché of the fierce, dangerous shifter.

Iannis's eyes widened in warning, and I grinned at him right before snapping my fingers. The storm abruptly stopped, and with another spoken Word and a wave of my hand, the room was put back to normal. The crowd murmured in amazement as the dishes righted themselves, the wine glasses refilled, and the curtains once again hung from their rods, intact and untorn. Not a single hair was out of place on a lady's head, not one thing in the room broken. Putting the room back together was far more difficult than destroying it, as any trained mage would appreciate, but with Fenris's knowledge and my own magic, I'd done it flawlessly.

I bowed, and after a split second, the room erupted into applause. Iannis's eyes were twinkling as I rejoined him at the table, and I kissed him on the cheek before leaning over to meet Lady Porgillas's shocked face.

"I apologize if I frightened you," I said, loud enough that my voice carried. "I'm afraid I don't quite know my own strength sometimes."

"Oh, no need to apologize," the lady said, waving my words away with a delicate hand. "You fixed all the damage, which is quite impressive in and of itself. You are a fine teacher, Lord Iannis."

We took our leave shortly after that, thanking Lady Porgillas for a highly interesting evening. As we made our goodbyes, several of the guests gave me anxious or leery looks, and I hid another smile. Word of this incident would quickly spread in their circles, and maybe at the next party the mages would think twice about insulting my magical prowess behind my back.

2

I breathed a sigh of relief as the carriage set off for our long ride back to Solantha Palace. Part of me wished we could have taken the steamcar, but these silly four-horse carriages were traditional when it came to attending high-society events. And besides, the ride gave me some downtime with Iannis without anybody else around to interrupt.

"I thought this evening would never end," I said as I leaned my head against his shoulder. "The sooner we get through the next few weeks, the better."

"I do understand how you feel about these parties," Iannis said lightly, rubbing my shoulder. "They are not my favorite activity either. But in reality, they only account for a fraction of your time. You've been able to get quite a bit done, haven't you?"

I nodded. "There's still a lot of work to be done on reforming the Enforcers Guild," I said. I'd presented my commission report a few weeks ago, and the recommendations were being implemented even now, albeit with quite a bit of foot-dragging and teeth-gnashing. "The veterans in the Guild aren't exactly thanking me either. They're still clinging to their stupid sense of entitlement, and hate that the wages of the younger enforcers have been raised more than their own."

"That's not surprising," Iannis observed. "Many people would rather pass up a raise than see somebody else get a bigger one."

"Well that's just stupid," I said, shaking my head. "And they still are not taking the new unit for fraud and financial crimes seriously. Without bounties dangling in front of their noses, a case is just not on their radar."

"Nothing worth doing was ever accomplished overnight," Iannis said. "It will take time to root out the corruption and bad habits, and it is especially difficult when top management is refusing to acknowledge the size of the problem."

"You're telling me," I said with a sigh. "I'll have to keep an eye on them in the meantime, and keep pressure on Captain Skonel to prevent backsliding."

We fell silent for a while, and I brooded about the problem for a bit longer. I'd gone from being the underdog at the Enforcers Guild to the unofficial top dog, and while some of the enforcers appreciated my efforts to even out the system, it was still a largely thankless job. I could see how leaders and politicians could easily become jaded fighting for people who didn't want or appreciate their help. It was a good thing that I had my friends to rely on, or I might have torn my hair out a long time ago.

"That was quite a show you put on tonight," Iannis said, interrupting my train of thought.

"Well, you did tell me that I could use higher-level magic," I said. "I think I made a good impression on the ones that still think I'm a weakling, don't you?"

"Yes, and you embarrassed that group of ladies tonight as well," Iannis said dryly. "While I appreciated the joke, and don't doubt those women thoroughly deserved it, such pranks are hardly worthy of you, Sunaya."

"Yeah, yeah, I get it," I said with a roll of my eyes. "We have to 'keep up appearances' and remember the dignity of your position."

"It isn't about keeping up appearances," Iannis said. "It's about learning to rule with a steady hand. You can't let your feathers get ruffled every time someone makes a snide remark about you, Sunaya. If I did that, I would have blown the palace to smithereens a dozen times by now."

I scoffed. "Give me a break, Iannis. *Nobody* makes snide remarks behind your back. All the mages love you."

Iannis's eyes narrowed. "Really? You think that all my staff are pictures of adoration at all times? That they never balk at my orders, or give me the side-eye when they think I'm not looking?"

"Maybe they do," I shot back, "but at least they respect your abilities. They don't consider you a weakling or a savage, and they certainly don't think that you don't *belong*."

Iannis sighed. Silence stretched in the carriage, and for a minute, I thought he wasn't going to respond. But then he said, "I do understand how hard it is for you. I might not have to deal with prejudice now, but I did in my far-off youth, and I didn't like it any more than you do now."

"You?" I stared at him. "But you were born into a mage family."

"Not a pure-bred one," he reminded me. "The Tua look down on all humans, mage or not. In their eyes, I was a bug not even worthy of being squashed."

"Oh." I blinked—Iannis almost never brought up his Tua heritage. The Tua were a mythical, powerful race of beings who existed on another dimension entirely, though they had been known to come to Recca every once in a while, and had inspired many legends. They were so powerful that humans didn't stand a chance against their magic, and whether an encounter turned out well or badly depended entirely on the Tua's whim. Manuc, the island country where Iannis had been born, seemed to be their favored spot in our world. But as far as I knew, even there Tua sightings were extremely rare.

"I didn't realize you interacted with them, other than your mother, I mean." Iannis's mother was half-Tua, and the source of his extraordinary purple eyes as well as his unusual magical power and longer than normal lifespan. "Have you ever been to the Tua realm?" According to all the stories I'd ever heard, humans who were carried off to that other dimension didn't return, at least not in the same century. But then, stories could be misleading, especially since, in this case, there weren't any first-hand accounts.

"I was taken there once, when I was very small," Iannis said, surprising me. "I must have been about five or six, and small for my age, as the Tua blood made me slow to mature."

"What was it like?"

He was silent for a moment, contemplating. "Very strange. For a young child, difficult to take in—everything was so huge, the colors were off, the animals seemed bigger and deadlier. It was both beautiful and terrifying, and gave me nightmares for years after, even though I only stayed for less than a day."

"What were you doing there?" I couldn't imagine why any parent would think it was a good idea to take a young child to a different, and not to mention dangerous, dimension.

"My mother went there to present me to our kin, on my grandmother's orders. But their clan head disapproved, we found, and told Mother to never bring me back. They said that I would not be able to survive the dangers, and they had no desire to be saddled with such a fragile, vulnerable burden." His expression was rueful, but I could imagine how he must have resented that verdict, even as a young child.

I snorted. "Burden, my ass," I said. "If only they could see you now."

Iannis shrugged. "The Tua have very little interest in our governments or countries," he said. "They would not find me impressive unless I ruled the entire world, and I have no intention of doing so."

"You better not," I warned. "I do want to see you *sometimes*."

Iannis laughed, kissing my forehead. We sat for a while in companionable silence, but eventually my mind began to drift again. I felt guilty for snapping at Iannis earlier—yes, I had to deal with some ragging, but didn't everyone when they were the new kid on the block? Once we were married, and my apprenticeship was officially completed, all that would die down. People in powerful positions always had to deal with criticism of some kind or another.

The problem was, I had never aspired to a powerful position or spending time in mage high society. I'd only ever wanted to be an enforcer, to serve justice to those who needed it and protect the less fortunate. That was why reforming the Enforcers Guild was one of the first projects I'd taken on, in addition to helping with the rebuilding and relief efforts after the big quake.

On top of all that, I was still in charge of testing schoolchildren for magical abilities—another round of testing was due in the fall, just a few weeks after the wedding. That was always an emotional time for the families and children concerned. I suspected that by winter we'd need a full school, perhaps a boarding school, for the talents we identified state-wide. Yet another job I'd have to supervise myself if I wanted it done right. It turned out that once I got past the annoyance of having to deal with multiple people, I was good at organizing and directing. At first, the mages who had been assigned to work with me didn't know how to react, but now that I'd begun to prove myself as a leader, everyone seemed to expect so much of me.

There were times that I wanted to tear off the fancy clothes and howl, to shift and run in my beast form and escape the endless formalities and duties. But I hated the idea of disappointing Iannis, not to mention everyone else who supported me. Shifter-town hailed me as a hero now—something else I was still trying to get used to—and Nelia, my secretary, sorted through endless piles of fan mail that came in from all over the country. I wondered if I would ever get used to all of this, if it would just seamlessly become part of my ever-changing life.

"Is everything all right?" Iannis asked, noticing my pensive mood.

I shook my head. "It's nothing."

He slid an arm around me, pulling me tight against him. "It's more than nothing. You look like you've been carrying the weight of the world on your shoulders."

I laughed a little. "Sometimes I feel like I am." I nuzzled his neck, taking in a deep breath of his sandalwood and magic scent. "I don't mean to complain, I really don't. You deal with ten times the amount of work I do, and you never whine about any of it."

"I also have centuries of experience in doing so," Iannis reminded me, kissing the top of my head. "And when I started, I wasn't nearly as good at it as you are. You have the right to be out of sorts as you adjust."

"But that's just the thing, Iannis," I said, lifting my head to meet his violet gaze. "I'm not sure I'll *ever* get used to it. All this high-society stuff...it's not for me. I miss my friends—I haven't seen Annia in forever, not since she went to look for Noria, and since I've got responsibilities I can't go looking for her. Rylan lives in the same damn town as me, and yet I rarely get to see him or Comenius. And Fenris..." I shook my head, not willing to go down that path again. "I hardly even see *you* anymore, Iannis." I cupped his cheek.

"I know it seems like it was an age ago, but we did have occasional free time before the quake, and we will again," Iannis said, running a hand over my curly hair. "Canalo has recently gone through turmoil, but it will settle down eventually. We're well on our way to restoring order, and once the wedding is past, we'll have more free time to enjoy each other. Our life together has only just begun, Sunaya, and with the Creator's favor, we'll have several centuries to enjoy it. There is still so much for us to look forward to."

"You're right," I said, smiling at the tender look in his eyes. "There is a lot to look forward to, and a lot right now to be thankful for. It's a good thing I have you around to remind me of that."

"Indeed." Iannis shifted, then pulled me on top of him. "I don't know about you," he said against my mouth, his hands sliding up my skirts, "but I can think of much better ways than mere conversation to spend the remainder of our carriage ride."

Laughing, I kissed him, and let all my thoughts drift away. I had said I wanted more alone time with Iannis, and with no one around to disturb us for another hour, I wasn't about to squander it.

3

By the time we made it back to Solantha Palace, it was close to two in the morning. Exhausted from the day's activities and our passionate lovemaking in the carriage, Iannis and I headed straight for bed, but we were waylaid halfway to his suite by Director Chen.

"I'm sorry to disturb you at this late hour," Chen said, a dismayed expression on her usually placid face, "but we've received an urgent missive from the Minister."

"So urgent that it could not wait until morning?" Iannis asked with a frown.

Chen pulled a folded-up letter from her sleeve. "See for yourself," she said, handing it to him.

Iannis unfolded the single sheet, and I peeked over his shoulder. "You've *got* to be kidding me," I grumbled, a headache pounding at my temples with each line that I read. The Minister had decided that he wanted to hold the Convention in Solantha this year, during the week immediately before the wedding, since nearly all the Chief Mages were coming here anyway.

Iannis groaned. "We've only a few weeks left before the wedding. He wants us to start preparing for a Convention *now*, on top of everything? Has he lost his mind?"

Chen shook her head. "The Minister is clearly thinking of no one but himself," she said, crossing her arms. "Yes, this might be more convenient for the other Chief Mages and save them a trip to Dara, but it is going to be a nightmare for those of us who have to organize the event with such a short deadline."

"No fucking kidding." I scrubbed a hand over my face, already feeling overwhelmed. "That means it's not just the Chief Mages coming into town—they're all going to drag their entourages with them, *plus* all the officials and media VIPs and lobbyists and all the other crap that comes along with the Convention."

"We might have been able to handle such an influx before the quake," Iannis said tersely, "but many of our hotels are still being rebuilt, and Solantha Palace does not have a meeting room large enough to safely hold the entire Convention."

That was an understatement. My shoulders knotted with tension at the thought of all these strangers descending upon what I was beginning to think of as my home. "We may have to hire cruisers again to accommodate everyone," Director Chen said. "Seeing as how we have very little time to make the preparations, I thought you and I should go over the logistics before we retire."

"As much as I would rather rest, I'm afraid I agree with you."

Iannis sighed, then put an arm around my shoulders and kissed me. "Go to bed, Sunaya. I'll join you in a little while."

"All right." I kissed him back, resisting the urge to protest. I knew Iannis liked this even less than I did, but with only eight weeks until the new Convention date, there was no choice. I had a feeling that what little free time we had was about to evaporate completely.

Disheartened, I trudged off to bed alone, hoping that Iannis wouldn't take too long. As I lay in the big platform bed, staring up at the ceiling, I tried to fall asleep. But despite my exhaustion, thoughts about the upcoming Convention plagued me. I knew from my experience in Garai that delegates were prissy and demanding—the Chief Mages and the other guests would fuss if they weren't given "appropriate" accommodations and service, or if any one of them seemed to get preferential treatment, as if Solantha Palace was some fucking hotel instead of Canalo's seat of power. I wondered what they would think if they were locked up in a tower room, as I had been when I'd first arrived here.

Oh, how far you've come, Sunaya, I thought to myself as I rolled over. I'd gone from sleeping in a dingy apartment in Maintown to the Chief Mage's apartments. I certainly had no right to complain about anything, even if said Chief Mage couldn't share the bed right now. In a few short weeks, this would officially become my bed too, and I could move my stuff from my suite down the hall to his.

"I just wish the Minister hadn't given us all this extra trouble," I grumbled out loud.

"Trouble!" my ether parrot squawked, materializing on Iannis's pillow. I laughed a little as he cocked his glowing head at me, and reached out to stroke his ethereal feathers. As usual, my fingers passed straight through them, but he leaned into my touch a little, almost as if he could feel it.

"Do you think I'm being crazy, Trouble?" I asked him. "Is it just pre-wedding jitters, or is this normal?"

"Crazy!" Trouble cawed back, and I rolled my eyes.

"Yeah, that's just what I wanted to hear." I flopped back down.

"Hear, hear!" Trouble hopped onto my chest and peered down at me. "Want to hear!"

"Want to hear what?" Frowning, I sat up a little.

"Wedding jitters!"

"You make no sense, you know that?" I shook my head, wishing that I could do something about it. Had I given him a little less of my power when I accidentally created him, he would have faded away as ether birds were supposed to; with a little more, he might be able to truly understand and respond.

Trouble came closer, attempting to burrow beneath my hair, and I sensed that he was lonely. "You okay, little guy?" I asked, petting his head and wishing I could feel his feathers. I wondered, not for the first time, if there was a way to improve Trouble without accidentally destroying him. I'd already tried it once in the past and had nearly unraveled the magical weft of his existence. Fenris's vast magical repertoire was no help, and Iannis had no idea what to do either. One thing was clear—I'd somehow bound up a bit of my essence into Trouble, which was why he was tied to me.

"Well, there's no point in worrying about what we can't change, right?" I said to the bird, snuggling down in the mattress. I pushed my hair off to the side, and Trouble settled right into it, like it was a nest. Being ethereal, he would not mess it up. The sight made me smile, and I was finally able to drift off to sleep.

———

GLOWING blue mist swirled around me, clinging to my shoulders and ankles, almost as if the very air was trying to cover me in a blanket. I squinted, trying to see through it, but I only caught glimpses of huge tree trunks, as wide as ten men, looming around me. Above, the night sky was a deep purple, with a round, green-tinged moon. The stars were all manner of colors, ranging from pure white to brilliant orange to pale lilac.

"Whoa!" I cried out as the ground shook and I was nearly thrown to the floor. I reached out to steady myself against one of the massive trees when a foot the size of a steamcar came crashing down next to me. Swallowing, I looked up to see a giant looming directly above me. He had long hair and gleaming sapphire eyes, but it was too dark to see his features.

His cave-sized mouth opened, and he spoke to me in a strange language, so loudly that it made my brain hurt. A clawed hand bigger than my whole body reached down to grab me, and I screamed, then darted away as fast as I could. I nearly ran straight into the outstretched palm of another giant, and as I shrank back, my heart hammering, I saw that what I'd seen earlier hadn't been tree trunks at all. I was in a forest of giants, and those gleaming stars were all eyes looking down at me hungrily, so hungrily...

"Stay back!" I yelled, conjuring a fireball. I shot it toward one of the hands, but the giant batted it away as if it were a fly. Strong fingers closed around my torso like a vise, and I screamed, beating at my captor with my tiny fists...

"Crazy! Crazy!" Trouble's voice startled me out of my dream, and I shot straight up in bed, my heart beating a mile a minute. Breathing hard, I clutched my hand to my chest and looked over at Trouble, who was squawking at me indignantly from Iannis's pillow.

"Sorry, buddy," I said, petting his head. "Didn't mean to give you a scare like that. Thanks for waking me, though." That had been one scary dream. I'd been totally helpless against those giants—not a feeling I relished, even if it hadn't been real.

The glowing bird squawked again, then hopped onto my shoulder and nuzzled my cheek. I smiled a little at his obvious effort to comfort me, but even as I leaned back against the headboard, I couldn't help but wish it were Iannis instead. A glance at the clock by my bedside told me it was after four in the morning—over two hours since I'd gone to bed. At this rate, Iannis probably wouldn't get a wink of sleep tonight.

Settling back down with Trouble, I wistfully thought back to that snowy mountain lodge Iannis and I had escaped to for an uninterrupted week of privacy in the middle of winter. We'd planned the excursion to coincide with my Heat and had enjoyed an incredible week rolling around in the sheets, on the rug in front of the fireplace, and especially in the hot spring in the backyard. It had been one of the best vacations of my life. My next Heat was coming up just after the wedding, during our honeymoon.

Maybe I'll forgo the special precautions this time, I thought. I hadn't thought much about having children, but the idea of a playful panther cub with Iannis's violet eyes was very appealing. Of course, there was no guarantee our child would be able to shift at all if he or she took after the mage sides of the family more. After all, Iannis was a full mage and I was half, so there was only a quarter chance that shifter genes would come forth. Though who knew, since mage-shifter unions were so rare and Iannis was not exactly a purebred mage either.

You should finish your apprenticeship before you have kids, a voice in my head suggested, and I sighed. That would be the responsible thing to do, wouldn't it? Luckily, I'd be able to finish my training much sooner than anticipated, thanks to Fenris's gift of knowledge...if I could get through all these damn events and obstacles that kept piling onto my plate.

The very idea was exhausting, and finally, my eyelids began to droop again. I stroked Trouble's head one more time, then slipped back into sleep, hoping I could get in a few more hours nightmare-free.

4

The next morning, I woke up refreshed and ready to tackle the day. Yes, the Minister had just given us a giant pain in the ass by scheduling the Convention like that, but at least this time we weren't battling to save the Federation from a deadly disease, or foiling an assassination attempt. In some ways, that stuff was easier than dealing with politics, but not having to worry about loss of life was a nice change.

I showered, then wrapped myself in a bathrobe just as a servant knocked on our door, bringing breakfast at the same time as usual. Whenever possible, Iannis and I shared our morning meal in the suite before starting our day. There was more food than what I usually ate on the platters the servant rolled inside, but I was confident I could polish it off on my own.

Iannis arrived when I was only a few bites into my meal, and there was plenty left for him. "Thank the Lady for hot coffee," he groaned, sitting down in the chair across from me. He took the pot that the server had brought up with the trays and poured himself a large cup.

"You look like you've been having a fun time," I observed over my forkful of sausage. Iannis usually looked fresh as a daisy regardless of sleep, but this morning there were faint lines of strain on his face, and his long red hair actually looked a bit frazzled. "You sure you don't need to catch some sleep?"

He shook his head, then took a long drink from his cup. "Just caffeine and good food," he said, and began heaping his plate with hash browns, bacon, and eggs.

We were halfway through breakfast when there was a loud *pop*, and suddenly an envelope appeared in the middle of the table. "What the hell is that?" I demanded, jolting back and turning over my chair at the unexpected intrusion.

Iannis stared at the envelope, his face turning paler than usual. "There is only one person who has ever sent me letters in this manner," he said, gingerly picking up the envelope.

"And who is that?" I demanded.

"My mother."

My mouth dropped open as Iannis ripped open the envelope. "Your *mother*?"

"Ennartha ar'Sannin," he said, unfolding the letter. "I haven't heard from her in over half a century. Fifty-three years, to be precise."

"She sounds like a doting mother," I said dryly, righting my chair and sitting down again. "Why is she contacting you now?"

Iannis read the letter silently, his expression growing more and more ominous with each passing second. His brows contracted, and his lips pressed tightly together. "What is it?" I asked, seriously worried now. Not many people could affect Iannis's cool like that.

"My mother has heard about our upcoming wedding. She is scolding me for not consulting her about such an important decision," Iannis said flatly. "She also says that while *she* does not personally object to our match, and my Aunt Deryna actually seems to be looking forward to it, my grandmother is furious that she did not receive an invitation."

I frowned. "An invitation? But I thought you sent one to your family?" And was that his evil Tua grandmother? If so, I certainly would not have invited her or dreamed that she would consider attending. From what Iannis had told me, his grandfather had been kidnapped and bespelled by a Tua against his will, then sent back with his infant daughter when his kidnapper lost interest in them. Really, where did she get the nerve to consider herself part of the family, after that?

"There are not many family members left in Manuc." Iannis sighed. "My father died three centuries ago—I wish he were still alive, he'd have loved you. I did send an invitation, of course, but it was a single invitation sent to my aunt's home, since Deryna is the only relative who maintains a permanent residence anymore. I asked her to pass it along to any others interested in attending—there are some cousins, but I don't even know if they are still alive."

"That sounds reasonable to me." The invitations *had* gone out a good six months ago—surely they could have responded by this point.

"One would think so, but my grandmother appears to be offended that I did not send an invitation specifically addressed to her. As if I could possibly have one delivered to the Tua realm!" Iannis sounded exasperated. "She demands that we come to meet her in Manuc immediately and halt all preparations for the wedding until she has given her verdict. My mother strongly advises me to comply with this edict, but then, she never could stand up to my grandmother."

"Are you fucking serious?" I asked, incredulous. "I thought the Tua kicked you out when your mother brought you to visit that one time, as a young child. How does your grandmother expect you to consult her when she lives in a different dimension? Have you ever even seen her?"

"I did meet my grandmother on several occasions," Iannis admitted, picking up a scone. "None of which ended cordially or endeared us to each other. In fact, she is the reason I left Manuc in the first place. I attempted to make a political career there in my younger years, but my grandmother ruined that for me. She demanded that I free a convicted criminal whom she favored for some reason, and when I refused, she destroyed the entire prison and took the fellow away. That was four hundred years ago, and she's yet to forgive me for not jumping to do her bidding."

"And she wonders why she didn't receive a wedding invitation," I said with a snort. "She sounds like a real piece of work."

"Yes, as vindictive and capricious as they come," Iannis said. "But even if we wanted to obey this summons—which I certainly do not—it is impossible for us to drop everything and go to Manuc on such short notice, especially with the added responsibility of hosting the entire Convention. I'll write back immediately and send my politest regrets, as well as a promise to visit at some point after the wedding."

"Are you sure that's going to be enough?" I asked dubiously. "If your grandmother is a Tua, and she's as capricious as you say, she might just decide to crash our wedding."

Iannis shook his head. "Hardly. My grandmother despises Recca and its inhabitants. She considers us uncouth and beneath her notice—Manuc is the only area she's been able to tolerate even for short visits. She won't care to set foot in the Northia Federation, no matter how angry she is at me. That would be too much of an inconvenience."

"Well that's a relief." I wasn't exactly looking forward to meeting this evil old bat.

"We can always visit Manuc in a century or two," Iannis suggested, "which is not that long in Tua eyes. By then her dudgeon may have subsided, or she'll be off-world again, and we'll have, most unfortunately, missed her."

"One can hope." Even if we did have to meet her, by then we'd have a baby in tow. From what I'd always seen, cute little babies were remarkably good at defusing family grudges.

A knock came at the door, and my cousin Rylan strolled in. "Sorry to disturb your morning," he said, dropping into the chair next to me as I stared at him in surprise. "I ran away from home and have no one to turn to." He gave me a lopsided grin.

I scoffed. "Nice to see you too," I said, ruffling his hair. "How'd you get up here?"

"Are you kidding? I know all the guards on a first-name basis thanks to my stint as your bodyguard." Rylan plucked a grape from the bowl on the table and popped it into his mouth. "You got any more food around here?"

Iannis raised his eyebrows. "I'll leave you two to catch up," he said, rising from the table. "Come find me when you're done, will you?" He leaned down to give me a peck on the cheek. "I'll be in my office."

"Love you," I said as he left. Once the door was closed, I handed Rylan the grape bowl. "You got tired of living with Aunt Mafiela?" I asked. "I'm not exactly surprised."

"I was this close to ripping every single hair out of her blonde head," Rylan grumbled as he plucked another grape from the bowl. "I'd forgotten just how bossy Mother can be. It is impossible to please her and keep my self-respect at the same time. I've saved up enough money—it's time for me to find my own place and make my own way in the world again. Where was that apartment complex that you used to rent from in Maintown? Your place was pretty nice."

I shrugged. "The building caught fire last time I was there, and after the quake, I've got no clue if it still exists. You can stay here for a few days, but you'll have to find something else soon because we're about to get a whole influx of guests."

"For the wedding, right?" Rylan shook his head. "I still can't believe that's coming up so fast."

"Not just the wedding," I said. "Turns out the Minister decided to hold the entire Convention here, the week before."

"The Convention?" Rylan's eyes widened. "Oh hell no. I'm sorry, Naya, but I am not going to be here for that, bowing and scraping to self-important Chief Mages and their staff. I've got some out-of-town business I've been meaning to do, so I'll make myself scarce until the wedding."

I laughed. "I never thought I'd say this, but I envy you right now, Rylan. I wish I could just up and disappear. Instead I have to deal with whiny politicians, and now Iannis's relatives too."

Rylan raised an eyebrow. "Iannis's relatives? I didn't know he had any that were living. Are they coming to the wedding?"

I shook my head. "We invited them, but somehow we didn't manage to get an invitation to Iannis's grandmother, and she's pissed about it." I gave him an abridged version of the letter, leaving out the part about his grandmother being a Tua. That was a closely guarded secret, and few people knew about Iannis's mixed heritage.

"Sounds like a bunch of nut jobs," Rylan said when I'd finished. "Complaining about not being consulted, after being out of touch that long? I wouldn't worry about it. Obviously, they're busybodies with nothing better to do."

"I know." I scraped my hands through my hair. "It just seems like these issues keep piling up, one after the other. I might lose my mind if I get any more bad news."

"Hey." Rylan punched me lightly in the arm. "All that stress isn't good for you. When's the last time you sparred?"

I blinked. "Uhh…" I trailed off as I tried to remember, but I came up blank. Had it been a month? Three months?

"Exactly." Rylan grabbed my elbow and hauled me up. "Come on, cousin. Let's go find that old training room of yours. Time to get rid of that stress the old-fashioned way. And besides," he added with a quick jab to my face that I barely ducked, "you're getting slow. At the rate you're going, Melantha will be able to knock you on your ass."

"Shut up," I growled, jabbing back at him. Melantha was Rylan's older sister, and she was even prissier than Mafiela. Rylan easily sidestepped my punch, then darted out the door, laughing. I chased him all the way to the training room, my blood already pumping in anticipation. I tackled him the moment we were inside, and we went down in a tangle of limbs, fighting to get inside each other's guard. Choking out Rylan might not solve my problems, but it would get some of this pent-up aggression out of my system, and I was a big believer in taking whatever I could get out of life.

5

My morning training session with Rylan was exactly what I needed. We spent a good hour trading between boxing and weapons, and by the time I rushed back to shower and change for my meeting with Nelia, I was feeling a million times better than I had last night.

Of course, some of that old pressure and resentment settled back on my chest when I sat down in my office with my social secretary, who was fresh as a daisy and ready with her clipboard. I had a feeling it would be a very long time before I grew out of that. But at least facing the day's work was bearable now.

Nelia started by reporting on the guest list—acceptances were still coming in—and all the new presents that had arrived since the previous morning.

"The High Mage of Castalis sent a replica of a famous portrait in his family's possession," she recited, as she went down the list.

"Of his ancestress, the daughter of the First Mage herself, with a jeweled frame. I wonder why he picked that?"

"Not many portraits have survived the Conflict, so it's of historical interest," I said. Fenris would be fascinated to see it, if he ever came back. "I'll write back to thank the High Mage personally. Bring the portrait here tomorrow and we'll find a good place to display it." This was my own ancestress too, and I was curious to know what she had been like. I wondered where the hell they were putting all the other gifts—was there a mountain of them stashed in a hidden room somewhere, just waiting to crash on top of someone like an avalanche if they opened the door?

"We're going to have quite a busy month ahead of us, aren't we?" Nelia said once we'd gone through the rest of the list. "Not only with the wedding, but the Convention now coming to Solantha."

I held in a sigh at the sparkle in Nelia's eyes—I wished I could share in her excitement, but it still all sounded like one big nightmare to me. "I imagine I probably won't see Iannis at all until our wedding day," I said mulishly, picking at one of my nails. "But at least I won't have to get involved with the political stuff." Or so I hoped.

"Do you think we should invite some of the officials to stay at the palace?" Nelia asked.

"The Minister should definitely get an invite," I said grudgingly —as much as I didn't like him, he was Iannis's "boss," for lack of a better term, and had stayed with us before, on his way to Garai. "There are a few Chief Mages we've worked with on fighting against the Resistance who probably also deserve an invite."

"While part of me agrees with you," Nelia said cautiously, "it is very possible that you may slight the rest of the Convention if you only invite some of the Chief Mages and not others. Since the palace doesn't have enough large guest apartments to host all of them, plus the families they may be bringing to the wedding, it is probably best not to extend invitations to a select few. Though you could still send one to the Minister."

I barely stopped myself from rolling my eyes. "Right. I forgot how touchy these guys can be, always ready to take offense where none was intended. I guess we can invite close friends and family to stay? Not that a lot of people will be taking us up on that—they all already live in the city."

A small shiver went down my spine as I remembered Iannis's Tua relatives, but I pushed that aside. They weren't coming out here—they'd made that clear. There was nothing to worry about.

"I have to admit that I'm glad Thorgana is dead and gone," I went on. "With so many important people gathered in one place, these events would offer a prime target for the Resistance. If she were still lurking here, as she had in the months before the quake, I shudder to think what she could do."

Nelia nodded. "Very true. Luckily, without a mastermind to lead them, these days the Resistance is a snake with its head chopped off. There are only a few rabble-rousers left, scattered across the country. Between the Enforcers Guild and Director

Toring's security team, we should be able to fend off any threats."

Right. I'd forgotten that Garrett was coming, but of course he would—he would have been in charge of Convention security in Dara, so it was only natural that the Minister would put him on the same job here. That meant he would arrive well before the others. "How many agents is the director bringing?" I asked. "Do we know yet?"

"A few dozen, I understand."

"He'll need them," I said, looking out the window at the city, which was still being rebuilt. Solantha had come a long way from the piles of rubble that portions of the city had been reduced to during last year's big quake, but there were still plumes of black smoke coming up from various parts of the city where steamtractors and other machines were hard at work reconstructing buildings that we had not managed to properly secure in time. "We're already crowded as it is—with the influx of guests and officials, Garrett will have his hands full. And the enforcers will be working lots of overtime." Maybe, I reflected optimistically, that extra income would help ease the jealousy between the older and younger crews.

Moving on, Nelia flipped to another sheet of paper on her clipboard and read the day's headlines to me. With so much to do, I had no time to listen to broadcasts or peruse the news, so Nelia did it for me every morning, then gave me the highlights. As she read them off, I gradually grew more and more annoyed—the newspaper and tabloid headlines had taken a sour turn lately.

When Iannis and I had first announced our engagement, they'd written up the whole thing as a touching romance. Our epic love had been a beacon of hope, proof that two people from vastly different classes and races could come together and make the world a better place. But someone at the *Herald* must have gotten a bug up their ass, because a few weeks ago they'd published an article saying that Iannis was cradle-robbing. The rest of the human papers had followed suit, and now there was an article popping up nearly every day questioning the suitability of our match. Paparazzi were following us around everywhere, to the point that I rarely left the palace anymore unless I was in disguise. While the papers pretended to champion me, they also threw out subtle digs about the disparity of power between Iannis and me, and made me sound like a poor little orphan girl with no family to support me.

"Isn't there anything we can do to set the record straight?" I finally asked, my voice simmering with frustration. "I'm getting really tired of the media taking potshots at Iannis and me. Magorah knows we're not perfect, but this is getting ridiculous! Honestly, who gives a shit about our age difference anyway?"

Nelia sighed, tucking a strand of hair behind her ear. "I'm afraid there's little you can do without making it worse," she said. Since she used to be a journalist herself, I trusted her insight. "The papers always spin things the way they like—they may say that they're here to report the facts, but ultimately sales are the driving factor, and sometimes just their own bias. The best you can do is keep your head down. This will all be over soon enough, and before you know it, you'll be enjoying a blissful honeymoon with your new husband while they harass someone else." She winked at me.

The thought of actually getting away from all this for a few weeks with Iannis did lift my spirits. I held the image of the two of us frolicking on a secluded beach wearing nothing but our skin close in my mind's eye as I suffered through the rest of my day, packed with meetings and tedious duties. By the time I'd finished with the last one, I was ready to curl up in my bed and shut out the rest of the world.

But I had one last appointment, and she was waiting in my sitting room when I entered. "Mrs. Lawry!" I exclaimed as the seamstress rose from my couch along with her assistant. "By Magorah, I'd completely forgotten."

"Which is why I insisted upon coming here rather than having you come down to my shop for your fitting," the seamstress said, clucking her tongue as she rose. "My goodness, you look like you're about to drop. Do you need a few moments to refresh yourself?"

"No." I shook my head, looking toward the garment bag that had been carefully laid out on one of the couches, and then toward the kit on the coffee table that I knew was stuffed with sewing supplies. "We should just get this over with."

"That's no way to talk about the most exciting wedding dress of the century," Mrs. Lawry admonished as I began to shuck off my clothing. She and her assistant unzipped the garment bag while I stripped down to my underwear. "I must admit I had some misgivings about the design you settled on, but this is certainly my finest work to date."

"It *is* gorgeous," I said with a smile as I watched them pull out the dress. It was ivory silk, with a halter neckline that wrapped around my neck like a choker. The halter was embroidered with black lace, and that same lace bridged down the spine of my otherwise bare back, then merged with the train, which I'd made sure was detachable. That same lace covered the bodice, making it look almost like armor, and there was a leg slit in the front that allowed for easier movement.

The seamstress nudged me onto the stool she'd brought, and I held still as they secured the dress onto my body. It looked just how I'd imagined, fitting to my curves perfectly. There was nowhere to hide my weapons on the dress, but that didn't matter. Fenris's vast repertoire of magical spells included the magical sleeve pocket I'd wanted to learn for so long, and I kept my weapons in there now, along with a few other essentials.

"We'll need to take it in here a little," the seamstress said, pinching at the loose fabric around my waist. "You've lost some weight," she accused.

I winced. "I've skipped a meal here and there," I admitted. Or rather, I'd grabbed a handful of beef jerky or whatever else had been available. As much as I'd enjoyed breakfast with Iannis this morning, there were many days these past few months where we'd been too busy to sit down and enjoy a meal together.

"Well, you'd better not skip any more before the wedding," she warned as she began to stick pins through the fabric while her assistant fussed with my train. "With your fast metabolism, you'll become skin and bones, and that's hardly an attractive look for a bride."

"Yes ma'am," I said, studying my reflection in the mirror. Now that she mentioned it, I was looking a bit skinnier, and the shadows beneath my eyes weren't particularly flattering either. Makeup would hide most of that, but still, she was right. I needed to take better care of myself.

But how was I supposed to find time for that when the responsibilities just kept piling on?

Suddenly, I felt a mad impulse to rip the dress off and run away from it all. To escape to some deserted island like the one Iannis and I had made love on for the first time, and run wild and free. Perhaps I'd even run around in panther form for a good long while.

Remember the honeymoon, I told myself for the umpteenth time today. It was beginning to sound like a mantra. This would all be over soon. I'd been through much worse than this. Surely I could handle a wedding, right?

6

The next few weeks passed by in a blur of constant activity. I bore the stress of prepping for the Convention with a smile, determined not to worry Iannis or let anyone else know how much of a downer all this madness was. Thankfully, I had Nelia to help me juggle everything, and once I rolled up my sleeves and dove into this mess, I tackled things with a combination of ferocity and efficiency that surprised even me. The entire time, I kept my upcoming honeymoon in the forefront of my mind—the shiny carrot I was chasing. This hectic phase would be over soon, I reminded myself. Only five weeks to go.

"Miss Baine?" Nelia called through the telephone intercom to my office in the Mages Guild.

I bit back a sigh and answered. "Is the spokesman for the fire-fighter union here?" I asked. I was supposed to arrange schedules for setting anti-fire wards with him, freeing up the Mages Guild to deal with the tricky Convention logistics.

"Actually, he cancelled at the last minute because of a fire in some warehouse. Your next appointment was postponed too. You're free until four o'clock."

I blinked. Four o'clock? I glanced at the clock on my wall. That was hours away! "Thank you," I said with a grin. "I'll be out of the office until then."

I hung up before Nelia could respond, then bounced out of my chair and left the Guild. I couldn't remember the last time I had three whole hours of time to myself, and even though there was paperwork I should catch up on, I desperately needed the break. Rushing up to my room, I changed into a pair of shorts and an old but well-loved T-shirt, then called Comenius.

"Hey, Com," I said when he answered the phone. "Is Rusalia around?"

"She's off school today," he said. "Are you finally free to tutor her?"

"I was actually thinking more of a playdate," I said, "with her, Liu, and Tinari." I used to spend time with the girls every week before things got so hectic—I tutored Rusalia on controlling her magic, and in general I enjoyed playing with the high-spirited little girls. "Do you think you can bring her by?"

"She would love that," Comenius said as Rusalia squealed in the background. "She'll be at the palace within the hour."

I hung up the phone, then checked in with Janta and Mrs. Tandry. Liu was baking bread right now, but she'd be free soon, and Tinari was nearly done helping Janta catalogue a section of the library. They promised to send the girls straight to the play-room as soon as they were done.

With half an hour left until the girls arrived, I wandered back to the Mages Guild wing to see if I could catch Iannis for a few minutes. He'd already been up and gone when I'd opened my eyes this morning, and my serapha charm had told me he'd left the palace. But he was back now, and after barely seeing him for nearly a week, I missed him.

"Sunaya," Iannis greeted me with a smile as I opened the door—he was seated behind his desk, with a mountain of papers in front of him. His eyebrows rose a little as he took in my outfit. "Playing hooky today?"

I smiled back. "Two of my appointments cancelled, so I've found myself with a bit of free time. You?"

Iannis chuckled. "Free time is the last thing on my agenda," he said. "I'm glad you came by, though. I have good news. Fenris called earlier."

My jaw dropped. "He *did*? And you're only mentioning this *now*? What the hell, Iannis?"

"I got caught up in something!" Iannis held up his hands in a placating manner. "It was a very short conversation, so it wasn't as if I had time to get you. His friend was dying from a rare poison, and he called to see if I could give him the recipe for the antidote."

"Dying?" I plopped into one of the visitor's chairs, my head spinning. "What kind of trouble has Fenris gotten into?"

"I don't know," Iannis said, sounding frustrated. "But the lady in question sounded like more than just a friend."

I raised my eyebrows at that. "Are you saying that Fenris has a *girlfriend*?"

Before Iannis could answer, the phone rang. "Yes?" he asked impatiently as he snatched it up.

"There's a call coming through to your line from the same number Fenris called from earlier," I heard Dira say, and my heart leapt into my throat. "Shall I put him through?"

"Right away!" Iannis ordered. There was a click as Dira transferred the line. "Fenris, is that you?"

"Yes," Fenris's familiar baritone came through the line, and I felt a swell of relief.

"By Magorah, it's really him!" I exclaimed, leaning across the table. "Damn you, Fenris, for worrying us like this! Are you okay?"

"Yes, I'm fine, and yes, the antidote worked," Fenris said, and he sounded as grateful as I felt to finally hear his voice again. "I owe you a great debt, Iannis—Mina would have died today if not for you. I'm sorry I cut you off earlier, but time was of the essence."

"I understand completely," Iannis assured him. "You owe me no debt, Fenris—you have helped me more times than I can count. I am only glad that you and your lady love are safe."

"Speaking of lady loves," I said, snatching the phone away from Iannis. My throat was tight with emotion, and it took me a second to get out the words. "You've got to bring her to our wedding, Fenris. I don't care what we have to do to make it happen—I want you to be there. I *miss* you."

"I miss you both, too," Fenris said, and he sounded as if he meant it. "But I don't want to put you in any danger—"

"You won't be," I insisted, "and I don't want to hear any excuses. Give me your address so I can send you a formal invitation under whatever alias you're using."

Fenris laughed, a tinge of disbelief in his voice. "I'll get one from you in person, if I decide to go," he said, though he didn't sound very convincing. "If I end up unable to make it, you know that my thoughts and wishes are with you both."

"What happened with the poison?" Iannis asked, wresting the phone back from me. "Have you found out who is responsible? Croialis is not something that one could take by accident."

"We have suspicions, but no proof yet," Fenris said. "A large fortune is at stake, and greed is likely the motive."

"I know you can't tell us exactly where you are," I called, "but are you in any immediate danger?"

"No," Fenris assured me. "Mina is the target, not me. I will be taking extra precautions to ensure her safety, and we will be leaving here as soon as we've finished our business. I'll let you know where I settle permanently when it's safe to do so."

"Fine," I said, holding in a sigh. I wanted to know more, but I knew that this was the best I'd get from him right now. "But *please*, promise to stay in touch. I don't think we could handle it if you did another disappearing act."

"I'll do my best," Fenris said, and I could hear the smile in his voice. He was just as happy to hear from us as I was to hear from him, and I blinked back tears of relief and happiness. I couldn't force him to come to the wedding—I knew that—but just knowing for sure that he was alive, that he was safe...it took a weight off my shoulders that I hadn't even been aware of.

We finished up the conversation, and Iannis hung up with a smile. "I'm glad his lady pulled through," he said. "Fenris sounded distraught when he called the first time. Croialis is no joke."

"Me too," I said. "I don't think I could handle it if Fenris had found the love of his life only to lose her. He's been through so much—he deserves to be happy." Maybe Fenris wouldn't be able to come to our wedding, but I damn well intended to go to his. Once all of this was behind us, I was going to track him down so I could hug him in person and meet the lucky lady who'd managed to snag his heart.

———

I SPENT a few more minutes with Iannis, then went down to the playroom to meet the girls. The three of them appeared right on time, dressed in shorts or summery dresses, as I'd told their parents to make sure they were ready for some outdoor play-time. The playroom was an unused salon that I'd converted for the children, and it was filled with toys and games.

"Let's play tea party!" Tinari cried as she bounced into the room on Liu's heels. "We brought sweets up from the kitchen, so it'll be perfect!"

"Ooh," Rusalia said, her blue eyes wide as she stared at the platter of pastries in Liu's hand. "Those look really good. Did you make them yourself?"

"Yes, but they're for later," Liu said, lightly smacking her hand away before Rusalia could grab one. "I like the idea of a tea party. What do you think, Sunaya?"

"A tea party sounds great," I said, taking the platter from her. "Why don't you girls get the teacups and pot and we'll set everything up?"

The girls eagerly rushed to get the supplies, and I stood back and watched as they put out the lace tablecloth and tiny porcelain dishes. Liu, the natural ringleader despite her lack of magic, directed where everything should go, and I set the pastries on the platter she'd designated.

We spent the next hour having tea, all of us pretending to be noble ladies from various countries. I used the opportunity, as I did with nearly all of our playtime sessions, to teach them a little bit of magic. I conjured water into the pot, and Rusalia boiled it with her magic, while Tinari kept the pastries warm by heating the platter lightly. Liu had brought real tea leaves from the kitchen, and within no time she was pouring tea into the cups for us to enjoy.

At some point, Trouble decided to make an appearance, and the girls had fun chasing him about the room. He was a great favorite with the kids, and he didn't mind letting them try to catch him—they couldn't really touch him anyway, and he seemed to understand it was a game.

As I watched the girls play, I wondered if I would soon be playing with my own children. Now that Iannis and I were about to be married, having children seemed to be the logical next step, and with my Heat coming up on our honeymoon, it might be the perfect time to get started. But was this really the right time to do it, so soon into our marriage? Or did we need more time to settle into the new, strange life we were creating together? I'd have to talk it over with Iannis.

"Look," Rusalia cried, getting my attention. "I've been practicing my fire magic!"

I glanced up to watch her conjure a thin stream of flame, then shape it into a heart. "Good job!" I said as the other girls squealed. A spark jumped from the flames, alighting on a pile of cleaning rags on a nearby table. To my horror, the rags ignited, and the girls' squeals turned into screams as flames shot straight toward the ceiling. Rusalia lost control of her fire magic, and the next thing I knew the flames were spreading to the drapes and the carpet and were rapidly headed for a box of dolls in the corner.

"Get back!" I yelled, jumping to my feet. I shoved the girls behind me, then quickly conjured a wave of water. The water splashed over everything, dousing the fire in an instant, but leaving behind the strong reek of damp soot. Sighing, I pushed a hand through my hair and surveyed the damage. The curtains were beyond repair, as was the table those rags were sitting on.

The girls seemed unhurt, but they were sooty too, and Rusalia's skirt had been badly damaged by the fire.

"What happened?" Carlin, the butler, demanded as he rushed into the room. His eyes widened as he surveyed the damage, and he glared at the cowering girls. "Do you have any idea how long this is going to take to clean up?"

Ignoring him, I bent down to sniff at the rags, which had been burnt to a crisp. "Alcohol," I said, straightening up. "Whose idea was it to leave rags soaked in alcohol in this room?" I planted my hands on my hips as I stared down the butler.

"The playroom was not a priority, with all the guest rooms being readied," he said stubbornly, refusing to back down. Carlin was a holdover from the previous Chief Mage and had never liked me much. "And I hardly expected the rags to be set on fire. Someone should teach these children to better control their magic!"

"And *you* should stop acting so high and mighty before I decide to burn you to a crisp," I growled, stalking over to him. Carlin paled as I jabbed a finger into his chest. "You know damn well that this is the playroom and these children are still learning how to use their magic. Make sure the servants don't leave cleaning supplies or anything else dangerous in here again."

"Yes, Miss Baine," he said grudgingly, bowing his head. I resisted the urge to smack him across his judgmental face—clearly this man had either never dealt with children or had no patience for them. I was going to need to have a chat with the steward about this later—if my own children were going to be running around the palace someday, I definitely wanted to make sure their play spaces were safe. We'd need a trained mage nanny, I realized, or perhaps two, to keep up with them. And perhaps it was time for Carlin to retire to some beachside cottage. What kind of pension package did his job entail? One more thing to find out.

"All right," I finally said, turning back to the children. "What do you say we go enjoy the rest of our day outside?"

―――――

THE GIRLS WERE FEELING guilty and scared after the near-disaster in the playroom, but once I managed to coax them outdoors, they quickly forgot about the fire. Soon enough, we were engaged in a game of hide-and-seek. The vast gardens would ordinarily make it quite a challenge, but as I closed my eyes and counted to thirty, I could hear the girls giggling as they scampered off in different directions. I was going to have to make an effort not to find them too fast—I could ferret them out all too easily with my shifter senses.

"Ready or not, here I come!" I called, finally opening my eyes. The girls were nowhere to be seen, but as I stood up, my nose twitched, easily separating out their scents. I decided to follow Tinari first, whose scent was redolent of candy and book binding glue. Pretending to look around and search, I casually made my way around the side of the palace toward the rose garden.

On my way to Tinari's hiding place, I passed by one of the shallow pools dotting the palace garden. I stopped for a second to admire the glimmering carp swimming below the surface, then frowned as I realized I couldn't see any. Despite the bright, sunny weather, the water was an odd dark color obscuring the normally clear depths. Had somebody contaminated the water with some kind of dark ink? And what would that do to the poor fish? Drawing closer, I noticed a ripple near the edge closest to me, and the hairs on my arms rose as I scented a strange brand of magic. It was a lot stronger than the usual burnt-sugar smell, with an exotic undertone.

"What the hell is going on here," I murmured, bending at the waist a little so I could get a better look. I wasn't stupid enough to let the dark water touch me—if there was some kind of spell at work, that might not be safe. I was just about to call to the gardener when a giant pale hand shot out of the water and grabbed me around the waist.

"Hey!" I yelled, shock and horror filling me as I struggled against the fist. What the hell was going on here? I blasted it with fire, but the flames had no effect as the hand yanked me beneath the surface of the pool. The water was only four feet deep, so I expected to hit the ground instantly, but instead I was dragged deeper, and deeper, until the water pressure was unbearable. My head was splitting, my lungs were bursting for air, and there was only cold darkness. Not a single life form was around me aside from the giant fist crushing my ribs, not even the flash of a fish scale.

By Magorah, I thought dimly as I began to lose consciousness. My struggles grew feeble as I ran out of air and lethargy weighed down my limbs. *Am I about to die?*

7

J
ust when I was certain I was about to expire from lack of oxygen, the hand hurled me out of the water. I crashed into the grassy earth at full speed, and would have cursed when I felt my nose crack if I hadn't been so busy coughing up gallons of water.

"What the ever-loving fuck?" I managed to gasp when I'd finally expelled the last of the water from my lungs. Sputtering, I rolled onto my back and pressed a hand to my nose. It was already healing, but I sped up the process with a little burst of magic as I stared up at the sky. It was still blue, and the sun was shining between the puffy white clouds, but the air was a good twenty degrees colder and the scents around me were unfamiliar. What the hell had happened? Where was I? None of the magic I'd studied explained the trick with the giant fist, and there was nothing in Fenris's memories to explain it either.

"She looks like a drowned rat," a female voice sneered in a strange language, and I froze. Pushing myself up, I twisted around to see that three women were standing a short distance away, staring at me. There was also a little boy hiding in the branches of an old tree nearby. I'd been so discombobulated by my arrival that I hadn't noticed them at first.

"Who the hell are you?" I demanded as I struggled to my feet. Fenris's knowledge allowed me to understand her—she was speaking some version of Manucan, an old dialect. My shoes were filled with water, and my damp clothes were working against me. Scanning the area briefly, I saw that I was standing in the garden of an old country house made of gray stone, partially overgrown with moss and ivy. While it looked ancient, the mansion was in good repair, and the gardens had a variety of well-trimmed trees and bushes. Everything but the house and sky was in shades of lush green, and the air was damper than back in Canalo.

The three ladies standing before me were regarding me with various expressions of disdain or curiosity. The one on the right, silver-haired and hunched with age, seemed the kindest, her pale blue eyes shining with worry and excitement. The one in the center was middle-aged, and my eyes widened as I took in her silver-threaded dark red hair and her violet eyes. And the one on the left, who stood far taller than the others...

"I am Ta'sradala," she said imperiously, looking down at me from her straight nose. She wore a pale green gossamer gown and had long hair the exact same shade as Iannis's cascading around her willowy frame. Her shimmering violet eyes were narrowed with disdain, and her mouth was curled back into a sneer, but even these things did not detract from her ageless beauty. Her alabaster skin glowed as if power simmered just beneath the surface, and by the way the air shifted subtly around her, I expected that it did. "And you, little beast, are not worthy to stand before me."

"Let me guess," I said, crossing my arms over my chest and mustering all my bravado, because I was *not* about to let these women see that, inside, I was starting to quake in my boots. "You're Iannis's grandmother, and you"—I turned to the middle-aged woman—"are his mother."

"Ennartha ar'Sannin," she said, inclining her head slightly. Unlike Ta'sradala, her expression was blank, but I had no doubt that she wasn't exactly thrilled to see me. "Welcome to Manuc, Miss Baine."

"Welcome indeed," Ta'sradala scoffed. "We should smite her right where she stands. I will not allow such riffraff to mingle with my bloodline."

"Excuse me?" I snapped, taking a step toward her. My shock was quickly dissipating as fury took its place. "I don't care who you are or how powerful you are. You don't have the right to yank me from my home and then insult me on top of it."

Ta'sradala laughed, and the sound was beautiful and horrible all at once, like chimes that were out of tune. "You should be thankful you are not actually on my doorstep, or you would be dead," she said. "Though perhaps I will send you to the Tua realm, just to see if your feeble body can handle it."

"You two are being rude," the elderly woman chided, moving toward me. I stiffened, keeping my guard up, but I didn't scent any ill intent from her as she patted my arm. "I am Deryna, Iannis's aunt. My nephew has very good judgment—he must have seen something in you. I don't think we should be so quick to dismiss her, Ta'sradala," she said to the Tua woman. "Why don't we get to know each other before doing anything hasty?"

"I didn't ask for your opinion," Ta'sradala said coldly. "As the matriarch, I have the right to decide whether or not this... hybrid...is worthy of marrying my grandson. And so far, I am not impressed."

"And just how the hell do you know that?" I demanded, pushing Deryna's hand aside and taking another step toward Iannis's grandmother. She towered over me, at least eight feet tall, but I refused to be cowed. "You haven't stopped flapping your lips since you yanked me out of that pool. You don't know anything about me."

The air around Ta'sradala crackled with power as she bared her teeth. "Why you insolent little mongrel—"

"I'm a feline, not a dog," I cut her off before she could finish her sentence. "Not that it matters. Being called a mongrel would be a compliment compared to what I'd like to call *you*." My gaze fell on the little boy cowering in the trees, who looked terrified at the confrontation. Who the hell was he? But if I asked, I would call attention to the child, which I couldn't bring myself to do. He was pale and trembling.

"You are very impertinent," Ennartha said, speaking up for the first time since she'd introduced herself. She was frowning slightly now, as if not sure what to make of me. "While it is long past time for Iannis to settle down, I had not thought he would pick someone this raw and uncouth. Even a human might have been preferable. Still, perhaps we should let her speak, Mother. Since Iannis isn't here to shed light on the matter of his strange choice, maybe she can."

"Very well," Ta'sradala said. "Speak, mortal."

"What am I, on trial?" I glowered up at her. "I don't have to stand here and listen to this crap." I pulled the gulaya I kept for emergencies out of my magical sleeve. But before I could speak the Word to activate it, Ta'sradala flicked her hand and hit it with a bolt of magic. I stumbled back as a jolt went through me, and the hum of power from the gulaya died in my hand.

"Don't think you can escape so easily," she said. "Your magic is mere parlor tricks compared to what I am capable of."

I stared up at her, stunned. I'd never heard of anyone being able to disarm a gulaya like that before, and for the first time, real fear began to sink in. The Tua were legendary beings, seldom ever seen. Nobody truly knew what they were capable of, only that they were immensely powerful, and amoral by human standards. Could Ta'sradala really smite me where I stood if I refused to cooperate? Was she that cold? My intuition, and Iannis's warning, told me not to expect reason or mercy from her. Perhaps it would be best not to provoke her if I could help it.

"Good," she said, her lips curving into a satisfied smirk. "I can see you are finally learning to respect me. Perhaps you are not entirely witless."

That smirk ignited another spark of anger in me, and I did my best to bury it. "Listen," I said, splaying my hands in a placating gesture. "I don't want any trouble here. Iannis and I love each other very much, and I don't want to have any bad blood with his family. But you have to understand that if you hold me here and I don't show up for the wedding, it'll cause a lot of problems. Iannis will never forgive you, and it'll be extremely humiliating for him. We invited officials from all over Northia, and other countries too. Not to mention all our friends!"

"I don't give a whit about any of that," Ta'sradala scoffed with a wave of her hand. "The governments of mortals interest me little, particularly those barbaric places where Iannis has chosen to hide away. And while my grandson might be a little upset should anything happen to you, your relationship with him is but a brief moment in his long life. He will soon forget about you and move on to greener pastures."

"I wouldn't be so certain of that, Mother," Ennartha said cautiously, looking a little worried for the first time. "Iannis is far more attached to the human world than any of us have ever been. This is not the first time he has been infatuated with a female, and he does not react well to interference. I am not at all certain that this savage girl is a suitable match, but it is high time my son produced some heirs, so I am willing to let things take their course."

"You have always been weak and spineless, Ennartha," Ta's-radala spat. "*You* may not care about what happens to the family line, but I will not stand for it."

"And what does that mean?" Deryna demanded. "You cannot

mean to actually kill her, Ta'sradala. The poor girl has done nothing to warrant that!"

"Oh, I won't kill her," Ta'sradala said, her lips curving into a cruel smile. "The mortal shall be allowed to at least attempt to prove her worth."

"The *mortal* has a name, you know," I muttered, trying to hide my anxiety. Prove my worth? How in Recca was I supposed to do that?

"Ahhh, yes. What was it, Sumatra?"

"Sunaya," I snapped. "Sunaya Baine." I knew she was just baiting me, but I couldn't help reacting. I was soaking wet, had nearly drowned, and was a million miles from home with no easy way to get back.

"Very well, Sunaya," she said silkily. "I shall set three tests for you to prove your devotion to my grandson. I do not expect you to pass these tests, of course, as you are but a weakly shifter with a smidgen of magic. But I would be remiss if I did not at least allow you to *try*."

"How magnanimous of you," I sneered. I got the very distinct feeling that to Ta'sradala, who was probably quite jaded, this was just a cat-and-mouse game with a pre-determined outcome. She didn't really care about Iannis and whether or not he was muddying up the bloodline. "If you feel so strongly about keeping your family line pure, then why did you have a daughter with a human mage?" I asked pointedly. "Isn't it your own fault that your family line is all messed up in the first place?"

Ta'sradala's expression turned icy. "Don't presume to question me," she hissed, slicing her hand through the air. My throat constricted, and suddenly I was unable to draw breath. Choking, I clutched desperately at my neck, trying every spell I could think of to loosen this magical hold, but nothing worked.

"See? You are powerless beneath my might," Ta'sradala said, her eyes glittering with malice. Spots began to appear in my vision, and I slowly began to sink to the ground as my legs weakened. "Save your magic for the test, mortal. You're going to need every bit of it if you want to survive."

8

Ta'sradala made another gesture with her hand, and the next thing I knew, I was kneeling in a small, scruffy rowboat. Lightning arced across the stormy sky, followed by a deafening boom of thunder, and massive waves rose all around me.

Find safety, Ta'sradala's voice echoed faintly around me. *If you can.*

"Are you fucking kidding me?" I screamed as I realized the boat was riding straight up one of those waves. I grabbed hold of the sides and hunkered down as the boat crashed back into the next trough between the peaks, dumping buckets of water onto my head. Desperately, I used a spell to propel the water out of the boat before it could sink, then surrounded it with a strong air shield to keep more from getting in. The waves could try to batter it, but the shield would protect me from the worst of the damage and save me from constant bailing, which I'd have to do with magic since there was no bucket on board.

Panting, I looked toward the horizon, trying to guess where I was. Most likely somewhere off the coast of Manuc, and the position of the setting sun told me that I was headed west. East and south were my best bets, but I had no sail, and the storm was too strong for me to attempt to propel the boat in any direction other than where the current was pulling me.

As the waves continued to pummel my little vessel, I poured more magic into the shield to keep afloat. I wasn't a weak mage by any means, but I couldn't keep the shield up forever. Panic began to set in as the sun dipped beneath the horizon. Darkness would descend soon, leaving me with no visibility out here at all. An orca or a shark could come out of the water and try to make a meal out of me. I could only hope the water here was too cold for sea monsters.

Stop that, I ordered myself as I began to shake from the cold. Our high metabolisms meant that shifters didn't get cold easily, but I'd been out in the freezing water for too long, and I didn't dare take any magic away from the shield to try and warm myself up. *There must be something I can do.*

I took stock of the contents of my magical sleeve, hoping to find something that could get me out of this predicament. Unfortunately, I hadn't exactly packed in preparation for a stormy sea voyage, so there wasn't much. The novel I'd been reading would be soaked if I pulled it out, as would the blanket, and my weapons weren't going to do me any good against Mother Nature. I did find a water canteen, which was useful since Fenris knew a desalination spell to make sea water drinkable, so I filled it up. I also found a sturdy rope, which I used to lash myself to the boat just in case the shield spell failed and I was thrown overboard. There was also half a bar of chocolate and a crushed muffin, which I devoured immediately.

I need to pack more food in the future, I resolved once I'd swallowed the last mouthful. Back when I'd been an enforcer full-time, I had always kept a pouch full of snacks for when I needed quick energy. But living at the palace, with access to warm meals and unlimited snacks at any hour, had caused me to neglect to take emergency provisions.

Sitting back in the boat, I touched my serapha charm, wondering if Iannis knew I was missing. I reached for the bond between us, but to my alarm, I couldn't sense a thing. Had Ta's-radala somehow severed the connection when she had ruined my gulaya, destroyed the sliver of his essence contained in the stone? A surge of anger filled me at the thought—who did she think she was, interfering with Iannis's and my life like this? It was one thing for her to want to meet me, but to cut me off from him completely?

Would Iannis even know yet that I was missing? As busy as he was, he might not realize anything was amiss until he came to bed and I wasn't there. But no, the girls would have reported that I'd disappeared and raised the alarm. Maybe one of them had even seen what had happened. Someone had to have alerted Iannis by now.

I only hoped he was able to guess where I'd gone. Because if I didn't figure out how to pass these so-called tests, I was in *big* trouble.

9

Hours passed, with no end of this torture in sight. For a little while, the waves abated, and I was able to let the shield down long enough to dry myself, refill my canteen, and attempt a few spells. A location spell told me that I was indeed west of Manuc, but much too far from the coast. If the current kept dragging me in this direction, I was going to be hopelessly lost at sea. I attempted to redirect the current with another spell, but I couldn't do much—such magic required multiple mages, like the anti-storm spell that Iannis and I had used along with eight other mages during our voyage to Garai.

I did manage to lure some fish close enough to catch them, and I shifted into beast form so I could eat them raw. They helped keep the gnawing hunger at bay for a while, but even so, I was exhausted from my magical exertions. Putting the shield back up, I curled up inside the bottom of the boat and did my best to get some sleep. The sun rose and fell again as the endless hours passed, and I dozed uneasily, unable to sleep for fear that another storm might strike, or that I might actually come close to some land and miss it. Though from Fenris's geographical studies, this part of the ocean was too deep for any islands—the closest one was a thousand miles to the south.

Part of me wondered if crying uncle would end this madness, if the old Tua would hear me and transport me back to Manuc. But no, she would probably let me suffer out here until my magic was depleted and the sea ended up drowning me. That old crone was as vindictive as they came, and for whatever reason, she had it in for me.

Besides, it wasn't like me to give up. I might be miserable, but I wasn't desperate yet. I wasn't going to give in just because I was afraid, and I damn sure wasn't going to drown out here like an unwanted kitten. If I was going to go out, I would do it fighting, and I sure as hell wasn't going to give that bitch the satisfaction of hearing me beg for mercy.

———

SEVERAL HOURS PASSED, and the weather gradually worsened again. Just as I was about to resign myself to yet another day at sea, I noticed a weak, far-off light. It flickered and disappeared several times, but it was definitely there. Could it be land? Or another boat?

Gathering what energy I had left, I rose a little into the air using the levitation spell to get a better view even as the waves drove the boat from under me. Squinting, I saw it was a fishing vessel just close enough to make out in the foggy dimness. Its sails were furled to ride out the storm as it bobbed up and down on the open water. My heart leapt in my throat as I realized my boat was being carried in the wrong direction by the currents, and the fishing boat would no longer be visible within minutes. As I tried to decide if I had enough magic left to reach the boat with levitation, a huge wave slapped into me from behind, dragging me back into the icy water.

"Fuck!" I sputtered as I came up for air. I looked around desperately for my boat, but it was no longer in sight. Grimly, I struck out in the direction of the fishing boat, hoping like hell I was going the right way. I couldn't hold out against this storm for much longer.

The waves were tossing me up and down like a toy, and my arms and legs burned as I fought against the strong current trying to push me backwards. Twice, I swallowed mouthfuls of bitter seawater. Only sheer determination kept me going, even though my body was crying out for me to stop, to let go. The actual distance wasn't too far, but for a soggy, exhausted swimmer, getting there was beginning to seem impossible. The cold numbed my muscles and fogged my brain, whispering that it might be easier just to give up. But I couldn't do that—Iannis would never find me if I let the waves drag me under.

When I was so cold I could no longer feel my arms and legs, the fishing boat finally loomed before me. But the deck was too high up for anyone to see me struggling in the waves, and the winds were too loud, so it would be useless to scream or pound on the side of the ship. Gathering the last of my strength, I levitated myself onto the deck, then collapsed, my heart galloping in my chest as I gasped for breath.

But there was no time for me to lie there on the deck, which was slick and reeking of fish guts. A sailor rushed toward me, eyes wide as he brandished a cutlass, and I had to roll out of the way to keep myself from being impaled.

"Wait!" I cried, springing to my feet. "I'm not here to hurt you! I just need some help!" By Magorah, could my luck be any worse? Instead of sanctuary, I had found more danger.

"Help?" The man narrowed his eyes. Thankfully, he seemed to speak Northian, though his Manucan accent was quite thick. "What manner of creature are ye, then? A sea witch? You won't fool me. Begone!"

I stared at him, noting that he was trembling despite his defiant words. "I'm not a monster," I said tiredly, leaning against the railing. My legs were shaking, and I had to hold onto it to keep myself upright. Playing up my exhaustion, I sagged, and tried to make myself look as helpless as possible. "I just want to go home," I said in a pitiful voice that I wasn't exactly faking. "An evil mage banished me here, and I nearly drowned. I'm so c-c-cold…" My teeth rattled, and I wished like hell I could conjure a flame to warm myself up. But I had no magic left, and that would only scare the sailor, anyway.

The sailor stared back at me for several long moments, weighing his options. "Wait there," he said in a wary voice. "I'll get the captain."

I sank to the deck, leaning my head against the wall and closing my eyes. If these guys wanted to gut me, then so be it. I had no strength left to fight back.

A few moments later, I heard footsteps, and I opened my eyes to see another man, presumably the captain, climbing up the wooden steps. He must have dressed hastily, from the state of his jacket and unbuttoned breeches. He held a mug of something hot in his hands, while the sailor came up behind him with a blanket over his arm.

"Well, I'll be," the captain said as I took the mug from him and he got a good look at my face. "A shifter, out here in the high seas? What kind are ye?"

"A panther," I gasped, taking the mug from him. It was some kind of tepid tea mixed with rum, but it was warm, and I sighed gratefully as I took a sip. "Thank you," I said as the sailor wrapped the blanket around me. My shivering was finally beginning to subside.

The captain opened his mouth, no doubt to ask what the hell I was doing out here on his boat. But before he could speak, an invisible hand gripped me, and I was unceremoniously yanked away. I screamed as the world streamed by in a blur, wind howling in my ears so loud I worried I was going to go deaf.

Suddenly, I came to a halt and found myself standing inside a living room. Iannis's three relatives were seated on the couch and armchairs, warm and comfortable, looking up at me with mixed expressions on their faces. My hands curled into fists, and the impulse to beat the hell out of Ta'sradala surged through me.

If I wasn't as weak as a newborn kitten, I might have actually acted on it.

"Well, well," the Tua woman said, rising from her seat. She didn't look at all happy to see me. "It would appear that you survived after all."

10

"Gee, thanks for the praise," I said sarcastically.

"That wasn't praise," Ta'sradala said tartly. Apparently, she had no sense of irony. "You still look like a drowned rodent, and you stink like one too."

"Well excuse me, your highness," I sneered, giving her a mocking bow. "I'm afraid I didn't have time to change my clothes after nearly being drowned at sea for two days." Or had it been three? I'd honestly lost track of time—for all I knew I'd been out there a fucking week.

"Don't test me, mortal," she said, her eyes flicking over me in a brief perusal. "You should count yourself lucky that I brought you back at all."

"Well of course you did," I said sweetly. "How could you test me again if you didn't?"

"I think Sunaya passed with flying colors," Deryna said before the Tua could lash out at me again. "She made it through the storm with her life, and relatively unhurt, too. That took guts and perseverance."

"She cheated," Ta'sradala said coldly. "If she hadn't come upon that fishing vessel, she likely would not have made it."

"How is that cheating?" I protested. "You never said I couldn't use outside help." Of course, if she'd bothered to spell out her "rules," I'd have told her I refused to play her ridiculous games. How was I supposed to win against brute power like hers?

"I think we should consider it a draw," Ennartha said. "I have to admit she did better than I thought. She has a poor grasp of magic but showed an undeniably strong will to survive." She regarded me with cool violet eyes that seemed to pass right through me, and I had to subdue a sudden desire to stick out my tongue. I felt like I'd been dragged into the principal's office.

"While you guys decide whether or not I lived up to your ridiculous standards," I interrupted, "is there anywhere I can grab a shower and a change of clothes? Or would you prefer I continue to drip all over your carpet and make it stink like a 'drowned rodent?'"

Ta'sradala gave me a cutting glare, but Deryna stepped forward with a soothing smile. "Of course there is," she said, taking me by the arm. "Let's get you cleaned up a bit."

Deryna led me to the bathing room, where I was allowed a few moments of privacy to soak in the magically filled tub and wash all the salt and grime from my body. As much as I hated my circumstances, I had to admit the hot water felt amazing, and for a few moments I let my troubles slip away as I let the bath do its magic. Maybe I could even raid the larder before Ta'sradala sent me off to whatever new hellhole she'd devised for me. I'd make damn sure I stuffed my magical sleeve full of as much food as I could carry.

After I finished with my bath, I donned the dress that Deryna had left—a shapeless cotton frock that was at least warm, though not exactly flattering. I considered magically changing it into something more stylish, but my energy was still low, and I needed to conserve it for something more useful.

With a growling stomach urging me on, I snuck back down the stairs to loot the kitchen. Thankfully it was not near the sitting room, and I was able to slip in without alerting Ta'sradala or the others. I had no doubt that the bitch would try to starve me if she knew I was going after food, simply because it would increase my chances of failing.

How in Recca could this awful woman be related to Iannis? She was one of the most vindictive, heartless people I'd ever had the misfortune of meeting. And her daughter didn't exactly give me the warm and fuzzies either. Iannis, while stern at times, still had a heart. He had compassion, and more often than not tried to do the right thing. He didn't toy with people's lives simply because he had nothing better to do.

As I approached the kitchen, I heard the sound of a knife chopping against a cutting board and scented two people inside. Pushing open the door, I saw a wizened old cook with a large apron over her gown. She was slicing bread, while the little boy I'd spied earlier in the garden was sitting on a stool, gnawing at a slice of that bread and a hunk of cheese. The kitchen was old-fashioned in a charming sort of way, with garlands of dried herbs and garlic hanging from the ceiling, faded wooden cabinets, and even a wood-burning range stove. The pantry door was propped open, and my mouth watered at the smell of dried meats and cheeses.

"Can I have something to eat, please?" I asked as I closed the door behind me.

The cook lowered her knife and regarded me with suspicion. The boy was staring at me, wide-eyed and fearful. His throat moved as he swallowed, and I scented his anxiety. I wondered once again who he was—unlike the old ladies, he wore simple clothing, and yet he didn't seem to be a servant either. He had sad, lonely eyes and was far too skinny for his age and height.

"I'll have to ask the mistress first," the cook said. "Let me check with her."

I stifled a groan as she left the room—couldn't she have given me a bit of bread, at least? Were her hands really tied that tightly? I wondered which of the women was the "mistress" here. Was it Deryna, or Ennartha, Iannis's mother? Surely it wasn't his grandmother—she'd made it clear that she didn't actually live in the human world. She probably had a grand mansion or castle in the Tua realm and considered this country house little more than a hut.

With nothing to do but listen to my stomach growl, I approached the boy. "Don't worry," I said as he shrank back. "I'm not going to hurt you. My name is Sunaya. What's yours?"

"Drawe," he mumbled, looking up at me through lowered lashes. His eyes were blue, like Deryna's, but he had a mop of dark red hair, like Iannis, and there was something in the shape of his nose and chin that reminded me of him too.

"Who are your parents?" I asked, a little suspicious now. Could it be that Iannis had a son that he'd never told me about? But no, he wouldn't keep something like that from me. We were about to be married. I didn't expect him to tell me everything about his life, not when he'd lived for nearly eight hundred years, but surely he would have divulged something that important. Besides, he wasn't the kind of man to leave a child behind, out of sight and out of mind. He took his responsibilities seriously.

Right?

The boy merely shook his head and went back to his hunk of cheese. I tried to coax some information out of him, but either he was too afraid to speak to me or he'd been ordered not to. Sighing, I gave up and went to raid the larder. The cook had been gone for several minutes, and if I didn't eat something soon, my stomach was going to devour itself.

Drawe watched with wide eyes as I made short work of a large ham, several sausages, and an entire cherry cake. I offered him a piece of the cake, which he took after a brief hesitation, though he still wouldn't speak to me. That was fine. I would find out the truth about him eventually, from Iannis himself, or perhaps from Deryna if I could get a moment alone with her. In the meantime, I replenished my canteen, then tucked some dried meat, bread, and cheese into my magical sleeve without even a shred of guilt. Since they'd abducted me, I reasoned, the least these women could do was feed me.

I was just screwing the cap back onto my canteen when the door banged open and Ta'sradala stormed in. "Who gave you permission to eat?" she thundered, her face red with anger. Before I could answer, she immobilized me with a slice of her hand, then used her magic to yank me into the living room. The little boy cried out behind me, but there was nothing he could do, and I hoped he stayed in the kitchen. The last thing I needed was for him to face this old biddy's wrath.

Ta'sradala stared down at me for one long, terrifying moment, and for a minute, I thought she intended to leave me standing like a statue in the middle of the room all night. The other two women were absent—nobody was here to naysay her if she decided to choke me again, or worse. Helpless rage filled me as I glared up at her—I hated feeling so powerless, especially in the face of a bully like this. Wasn't there *anything* I could do? I strained against her magic, but it was far beyond my strength.

Was this how normal humans felt when confronted with a powerful, angry mage?

Finally, the Tua made another gesture and released me. I nearly stumbled over the hem of my dress as my body began moving again, and I caught myself against the edge of a table to keep from face-planting. As I righted myself, I tucked away the canteen I was still holding and turned to face my persecutor.

"I have had enough of your bullshit," I growled up at her, my entire body trembling with anger. "You might be powerful, but you have absolutely no manners or sense of honor. You terrorize everyone with your power like some overgrown spoiled brat. It's no wonder Iannis never talks about you—he must be ashamed that he has to call you a relative."

Ta'sradala's eyes blazed. "A miserable mortal like you has no right to insult your betters," she hissed. "You're nothing but a mongrel, and now a thief!"

"Thief!" I spat. "A thief because I helped myself to some food? Technically I'm a guest here, which means that your family *owes* me some form of nourishment. You must actually be afraid of me," I taunted her, "if you're resorting to starving me. Maybe you're worried I might actually win this twisted game of yours."

"Pah! We'll see about that," Ta'sradala scoffed. "I've clearly been too easy on you."

She waved her hand, and the air around me began to stir. Before I could react, I was caught up in an icy whirlwind. My surroundings blurred, and I was forced to squeeze my eyes shut as dust began to sting them. Clenching my fists, I braced myself for the next challenge and hoped that Iannis knew how much I loved him. If not for that, I'd sincerely be reconsidering tying myself to him, knowing that such a hideous monster clung to his family tree.

11

B y the time the whirlwind died down, I was excruciatingly nauseous. Doubling over, I braced my hands on my knees and took deep, slow breaths to keep myself from throwing up. The last thing I needed was to lose my lunch after going so long without real food. Since Ta'sradala had likely thrown me into an even worse predicament than the last, I needed to keep my strength up.

When the dizziness and nausea had finally subsided, I slowly rose so I could get an idea of my surroundings. I blinked as I looked around—I seemed to be in some kind of forest, but there was something very odd about it. The tree trunks were purple, the leaves cinnamon-colored, and the air smelled very different from any forest I'd ever seen in my life. Looking up, I gasped at the sight of the sky—it was jade green in color, and the sun hanging above was bluish with purple overtones.

This must be the Tua realm, I thought as a butterfly floated past my nose. Iannis had been here as a child—no wonder he had been frightened. It was too strange and different. The forest shimmered in a thousand different colors all at once, and I had to look away as my eyes started to ache. Panic filled me as what little information I had on this place began to pop into my head. Most of it was of dubious value, based on ancient legends and scary tales. Yet there were common themes, like time passing differently. If I ever managed to get out, would centuries have passed? Would all my friends be dead and gone, including Iannis? Tears stung my eyes at the thought, and I angrily blinked them away.

There's no point in worrying about what ifs, I told myself firmly. For all I knew, I would only lose a week, not an entire century. It seemed increasingly unlikely that I would make it back from this ordeal in time for the wedding, but the important thing was to focus on actually *making it out.* I would deal with whatever came, when it came.

Fighting back the dread that seemed to have permanently settled in my guts, I cautiously made my way across the strange landscape. Spiders the size of my head wandered about the branches above, but to my relief, paid me no attention. Several times, I bumped into things that I couldn't see, and from the snorts and shuffles that I heard, I gathered some of the invisible obstacles were animals. There was also an ominous buzzing sound, likely from some huge insect, that I retreated from quickly, though I never caught a glimpse of the source. I wondered if most of the local animals were making themselves invisible to hide from a predator. In that case, invisibility would be just as useful for the hunters among them. What if I accidentally ran head-long into something that could eat or trample me? Then again, perhaps these creatures might be perfectly visible to Tua eyes, and the deficiency was in my own senses. Neither alternative boded well for me.

That thought made me slow down even further. Using a walking stick, I tested the ground in front of me and sniffed constantly. Between my nose and my hearing, I was able to discern when a creature was in front of me, and I started bumping into them less and less. Thankfully not *everything* was invisible—I caught glimpses of strange rodents scampering through the brush and birds of strange shapes and colors flitting from tree to tree. Part of me wondered if it was worth hunting any of the animals, but I hesitated to try. For all I knew they would be poisonous to my system, and besides, I still had *some* provisions.

As the hours dragged on, I began to wonder if there was any end to this forest. The sun was hanging low in the sky, well on its way to dipping below the horizon, and painting the sky in brilliant shades of indigo and red. Coming upon a small clearing, I sat down beneath a tree and pulled out a bit of dried beef from my magical sleeve. Perhaps I'd camp here tonight and continue on in the morning.

But continue on to what? I wondered gloomily as the forest gradually began to darken around me. Soon, the only light would come from the pinkish moon and stars that were starting to appear in the sky. It wasn't as if Ta'sradala had actually told me what I was supposed to do. I assumed the challenge was to get back to the human realm in one piece, but how the hell was I supposed to do that? Even if I had a working gulaya on me, I had no idea if it could actually transport me between worlds. And I had no way to charge it, so I couldn't test the theory even if I wanted to. Neither Iannis's lessons nor Fenris's vast magical repertoire gave me the slightest clue how to move between different worlds. Unless I was merely expected to survive for a certain period before being yanked back again, I was screwed. And after my recent confrontation with Ta'sradala, she wasn't likely to take pity on me.

I was just beginning to doze off when I heard something massive trampling through the trees. A low growl had the hairs on the back of my neck standing on end, and I slowly got to my feet, pulling a chakram from my sleeve. For a moment, I was afraid this was another one of those invisible creatures, but as it came closer, I caught a glimpse of a large animal with shaggy, neon-green fur and glowing orange eyes. It was about the size of a horse, but lower-slung and far more muscular.

"Whoa there," I said, holding up my hands as it came closer. I caught a glimpse of sharp tusks, and drool dripped from a maw of razor-sharp teeth. "You can back off. I'm not here to hurt you."

The animal let out a roar loud enough to wake the dead and charged. The ground shook beneath the pounding of its hooves, and I threw myself to the side an instant before it could slam into me. Cursing, I threw a chakram at it, but the beast was fast despite its size, and it ducked. I threw another chakram as the first one slammed into a tree, and this one sheared off a bit of its shaggy coat as it charged toward me again.

"For fuck's sake," I snarled, magic sizzling at my hands. I was tempted to light the great beast on fire, but I didn't want to acci-dentally set the whole forest ablaze. Instead, I leapt high into the air as the beast charged again, and landed on its back. I held on for dear life as the animal bellowed, attempting to buck me off, and it took a supreme effort for me to draw one of my crescent knives. But I finally managed it, and I drove the long end straight through the base of its skull.

The creature let out a death scream that curdled my blood, then collapsed to the ground. As its lifeblood seeped out beneath me, I remained perfectly still, straining my ears to see if the ruckus had drawn the attention of any other predators. But the forest was deathly quiet, and I could feel a hum of fear in the air.

Not my fear, but *their* fear. Satisfied, I dismounted the carcass. Good. If the other animals saw me as a predator, they would stay out of my way.

With nothing better to do, I sliced through the beast's shaggy hide, then cut away a steak-sized piece of meat. Using my magic, I made a fire, then roasted the meat. It gave off a strange smell, and had an even stranger taste, but one of Fenris's useful magical tests established that it wasn't poisonous, and soon I was settling back against the tree with a full stomach and heavy-lidded eyes.

With my magic replenished, I was able to set a ward around the clearing that would alert me if anyone tried to cross it. Under better circumstances I would have kept trekking on, but I hadn't properly slept in days, and my mind was fogged with exhaustion. Shifting into panther form, I climbed up into a tree and laid my head down on one of the thick branches. I fell asleep instantly, my worries disappearing as I reveled in the simple pleasure of a moment's peace.

———

THE NEXT MORNING, I breakfasted on a bit of cheese and bread as I watched a purplish-blue sunrise that took my breath away. Whatever the outcome of this adventure, at least I had seen sights few if any people from Recca had ever witnessed—I only needed to survive so I could tell the tale.

The local creatures were beginning to stir, birds twittering their alien songs, animals both visible and invisible scampering through the brush. To my relief, I found no signs that anyone had attempted to breach my wards last night. This place might be strange, but I was beginning to acclimate to the odd smells and colors, and after a night of sound sleep I felt better than I had in a long time.

Carefully, I continued my trek through the forest, slowly but steadily making my way along the paths. I noticed that while some of them were animal trails, others seemed to have been blazed by larger beings—some trails were as wide as highways. A flash of memory had me stopping cold in the middle of one of those paths. That dream where I was surrounded by giants…had it been merely a fantasy conjured by my mind? Or a premonition? Some of the details, like the different-colored sky, had been quite similar to this place. Were there giants in the Tua realm?

And why not? I thought as I forced myself to continue along the path. I'd already seen plenty of odd things—giants were hardly out of the realm of possibility. Still, the idea of encountering one sent shivers through me. I avoided the largest trails and urged myself to move a little faster.

The local sun seemed to take a little longer to rise to its zenith than it did on Recca, but without a watch, I could not be sure that my sense of time was on target. As noon approached, I spied a huge, tower-like structure in the distance, jutting high above the trees. My heart began to beat a little faster—was this tower someone's residence, or some kind of military outpost? Did I dare approach? If the inhabitants were hostile, it might be a mistake to draw their attention. The last thing I needed was to find myself in the clutches of another Ta'sradala. Given that she was the only full-blooded Tua I had ever met, it seemed likely that the other Tua were just like her: cold and aloof, viewing mortals as nothing more than playthings. I imagined they'd feel no more guilt about killing us than a human did about stepping on an ant.

And yet, as the tower drew closer, I rejected the temptation to pass it by. After all, how the hell was I going to get out of here if I just blundered about the forest? I had no idea where I was going, no inkling as to how to get out of here. Yes, maybe I would get lucky and stumble across some portal, but I had a feeling it wasn't going to be that easy.

If I wanted to get out of here, I needed some help. I had to take the risk. Maybe I'd lose my life, but that might very well happen anyway, if I didn't figure out how to leave this world and find my home. The beast that had nearly killed me the previous night was probably small potatoes compared to other monsters lurking here that I hadn't run across yet.

Slowing my steps, I approached the tower structure as silently as I could, one of my chakrams in hand. I might not have a choice, but that didn't mean I had to be an idiot. I'd scout out the area first, see what sort of creatures lived here.

A couple of miles out from the tower, the landscape began to change. The trees thinned out, and I spied purple rivulets of water winding their way across the land. Several times, I had to avoid patches of quicksand that attempted to swallow my walking stick. More than once, I found myself so surrounded by them that I was forced to levitate across to keep myself from getting sucked in.

My skin prickled with anxiety as I did my best to stick close to the trees—I felt far more exposed in the open than I had in the shelter of the forest. Thankfully, a grove of golden trees with bright pink fruit surrounded the tower, and I was able to take cover there. I expected there to be guards outside the buildings, but to my surprise, no one was around. Crouching behind a bush, I studied the unguarded entrance, wondering if there were any traps waiting to annihilate me the moment I came close enough. Did I dare risk testing it out?

"*Nachdan,*" a booming voice said from behind me, and I froze. Turning slowly, I gulped at the sight of two Tua and a blue lizard-like creature standing between them. How had they sneaked up on me so silently? The Tua towered over me, both at least twenty feet tall, dwarfing the lizard-creature, which was merely the size of a dachshund. The way its tongue lolled from the side of its mouth as it regarded me curiously made me wonder if it was a pet.

"Come again?" I asked faintly as I rose. These Tua looked quite different from Ta'sradala—they had silvery hair and skin like starlight, and were dressed in tunics woven from some multi-hued fabric that was constantly shifting in color. I had to squint just to look at them, and I felt a headache beginning to come on. Would I go blind if I stared at them too long?

One of the Tua laughed, and suddenly their brilliance dimmed to something more manageable. Now that I was looking at them properly, I saw that one was male, the other female. Their features were similar enough that I judged them to be relatives —twins, perhaps? Like the lizard, they were looking at me curiously, with no malice in their gazes. Maybe they thought I was some kind of exotic creature?

The female Tua spoke again, but the rush of words was too fast for me to make out, even if they hadn't been in a foreign language. No human had ever mastered Tua, as far as I knew. Frustrated, I made a helpless gesture with my hands, trying to tell them that I didn't understand.

"My name is Sunaya Baine," I said slowly, hoping that maybe they knew Northian. If not, I could try Manucan next. I gestured to myself as I spoke my name. "Who are you?" I asked, pointing to them.

The male said something to the female, then reached for me. I hastily backed away and found myself pressed up against a tree, heart pounding. I clutched the chakram in my hand, wondering if I dared risk hurting one of them, but the Tua only pressed his finger against my forehead and said something else in that strange language. Something in my brain shifted, and my eyes crossed as I swayed, feeling suddenly woozy.

"There," the male said, speaking perfect Northian. I blinked up at him, trying to get my bearings. "Your language is harsh on the tongue, but it is easier for us to learn it than to teach you to speak ours. This is my sister Arala, by the way."

"Now, Nalan," Arala said, nudging him gently. "There is no need to be rude; it is not her fault if her language is crude. What a fascinating guest we have! She is a very long way from home."

"Indeed she is!" the male said as the lizard scampered toward me. The animal sniffed at me with his broad snout, wagging his long tail, and I couldn't help but smile and reach down to pet him. His scales were smooth and warm to the touch, almost like silk beneath my hand.

"You are the first non-Tua we have ever seen in our realm," Nalan said. "How did you come to be here?"

"I was sent here against my will by another Tua," I explained as I continued to pet the lizard. He curled up near my feet, and I crouched down, deciding that there was no advantage to standing since the Tua dwarfed me anyway. "She wanted to see if I would survive the experience."

The Tua shook their heads at this, and the lizard made a disgruntled sound in the back of his throat. Was he able to understand me too? Perhaps the local pets were as superior to ours as the Tua were to mages.

"That sounds cruel and barbaric," Arala said. "We have not brought humans here in an age, precisely because they never survive very long. It is forbidden."

If it was forbidden, I thought morosely, *then why had Ta'sradala sent me here*? Did she have enough clout to flaunt her own realm's rules, as she did on Recca?

"I imagine the only reason you are not already dead," Arala continued, "is because you are not entirely human yourself. Our forests harbor many dangers."

I nodded. "Yeah, I can't imagine a normal human surviving very long." Annia was a good fighter, and very fast, but she would almost certainly have been gored by that beast last night. And the quicksand would have made short work of anyone who couldn't levitate. "Is there any way you might be able to help me get back home? I really would prefer not to die here, if possible."

The Tua exchanged glances. "We would like to help you, but the knowledge you seek is a closely guarded secret," Nalan said. "My sister and I would need to learn more about you first before we can consider sharing this with you."

"All right," I said warily. "What do you want to know?"

"May we...may we touch you again?" the female asked. "It is the best way for us to learn who you are."

My skin prickled at the thought—the sensation I'd felt when the Tua had plucked my language from my brain had not been pleasant. They might learn more about me than I was comfortable with. But did I really have a choice? And besides, once I got out of here, I'd never see them again. In a way, that was better than sharing my memories with another human.

"All right," I said heavily, getting to my feet. It wasn't exactly like

I had anything to hide anyway. All I wanted was to go home, and I was no danger to them. "As long as you promise not to use the information against me or others on Recca."

"We wouldn't do that," Nalan assured me, "but there are some Tua who might. I don't blame you for being wary."

"Well, get on with it."

Arala reached out and gently placed two fingers on the nape of my neck. At the same time, she linked her free hand with her brother's, while the lizard leaned against me. I expected the same strange sensation as before, but instead, she merely stroked her fingers down my spine in a soothing, repetitive motion. Slowly, the tension began to drain out of my body, and with it, I felt my memories pass from my mind into hers. It was a little disconcerting at first, but when I realized she wasn't stealing them, merely copying, I relaxed. What would these strangers make of my life in a totally different setting? Could they even understand our customs and values?

"There," the female finally said, removing her hand. "It is done." I looked up into her sparkling gaze. "What a fascinating creature you are! A shape-shifter and a magic user all at once!"

"You've had quite your share of vivid experiences for someone who has lived for such a short time," Nalan commented as he passed a palm over the lizard's head. His scales had turned bright pink for some reason, and I wondered if they were an indication of his mood.

"It would seem," Arala said, "that humans, mages, and shifters live life more quickly and dangerously than we do. I had no idea the barbarian dimension was so exciting."

"Barbarian?" I said, a little indignant, as the two began to talk excitedly in their own language. I was disgruntled that they were leaving me out of the conversation, but there wasn't anything I could do about it. *At least they weren't torturing me*, I thought as I bent down to pet the lizard again. He rubbed against me, loving the attention.

"We have never considered leaving the Tua realm," Nalan said as they turned back to me at last. "We were taught that the outer dimensions do not offer anything much of interest, or worthwhile challenges to our intellect. But now that your memories have shown us how rich and varied your land is, we may very well come and visit."

Oops. Could Recca survive more Tua visitors? On the other hand, these younger Tua seemed a lot more easygoing than Ta's-radala. I could imagine what a stir they'd cause in Solantha. Their size alone would cause a traffic jam.

"You are welcome to stay with me any time, provided that I ever get out of here," I said, smiling despite myself. These two might be giants, with powers I couldn't begin to understand, but their faces were lit up like two kids in a candy shop. "What's the deal with this guy?" I asked, stroking the lizard again. "I noticed that he changes color."

"His name is Broghan," Alara said. "He is terribly playful, and changes shape and color at least a dozen times a day."

At that, Broghan got to his feet. His form rippled, and I gasped as he changed into a miniature pony with silver fur and a purple mane. He whinnied as I touched his velvety nose, and then changed again, this time into a giant frog with orange and blue spots. I recoiled as his skin turned slimy beneath my hand, and he flicked me on the cheek with his sticky tongue right before changing into a baby dragon the size of a small dog.

"Amazing," I said as I scooped him up. He opened his mouth and belched a tiny stream of fire that nearly singed my eyebrows off before he curled up into my arms. "These are all animals from my world, although nobody has seen a dragon in ages. How is he able to do this?"

The Tua chuckled. "Changing forms and size is commonplace in our world," Alara said. "Although Broghan is special." They exchanged another glance, and I sensed there was some inside joke I wasn't getting.

"All right, well now that you know who I am, can you please tell me how to get out of here?" I asked, a little exasperated now. "I really want to get home."

"Why the hurry?" Nalan asked. "You only have Ta'sradala waiting to taunt and torture you again. It is really a shame that you have gotten mixed up in her games. Is this Iannis you wish to marry truly worth enduring her wrath?"

"Yes, he is," I said tightly. "And I'm getting really tired of everyone questioning my upcoming marriage." By Magorah, was this what I had to look forward to for the rest of my life? Even the Tua, who had little concept of our ways, thought that Iannis and I were a bad match.

"There is no need to get so angry," Alara said soothingly. "We will help you, but first you need to relax, because you'll have to be at full strength if you are to have any chance. Here." She conjured a mug out of thin air and handed it to me. "Drink this."

I wanted to protest, but it seemed unwise to refuse, so I took the frosty mug and sipped from it. The light blue liquid was both sweet and bitter, and quite tasty, so I gulped down another mouthful. Instantly, I began to feel wobbly, the world tilting around me as the colors and shapes began to meld into each other.

"What's happening?" I gasped, panic seizing me as I clutched one of the trees for balance. Had they accidentally poisoned me?

Nalan said something, but his voice was garbled, and I couldn't make anything out. The next thing I knew, one of them gathered me up, and I forced myself to relax. I would have to ride out whatever this was until it passed, and pray to Magorah that I hadn't misjudged the intentions of these people.

12

I woke up in a giant bed big enough to sleep at least ten people my size. By the light coming in from an overhead window, I guessed it was mid-morning, though with these strange colors it was hard to be sure. Groaning, I turned onto my side—the mattress was hard like a plank of wood, and my back twinged in protest. A snuffling sound got my attention, and I sat up to see Broghan curled up at my feet. He'd taken on the form of an adorable wolf cub, and when he opened an eye to look at me, I felt my heart melting despite myself.

Noting with relief that I wasn't cuffed or restrained in any way, I decided I wasn't in any imminent danger. My mouth was a bit dry, but the glass of water waiting by the bed quickly took care of that. As I considered whether to leave the bed and explore or wait for some sign of my hosts, I stroked Broghan's soft pelt. He rolled onto his back, begging me to pet his belly, then licked my hand when I complied. I was amazed by how accurately he mimicked an alien species—if I didn't know better, I might have thought he was a real wolf cub. Even the scent was correct.

After a little while, I got up from the bed and decided to look around the room. To my delight, I found a set of leathers and boots waiting for me, folded up in an oversized closet—an exact replica of my enforcer leathers back home. The Tua must have gleaned them from the memories they'd taken from me. It was definitely a good sign that they had gone to the effort to provide these, along with the human-sized glass and jug I'd drunk from. I put on the leathers and was delighted to discover they were even more comfortable than the ones at home. I marveled at the Tua's casual mastery when I noticed the jacket buttons were of gold covered with black lacquer and engraved with my initials.

After I finished dressing, Broghan led me down the stairs into a large room and toward what looked like the dining table, where the Tua were waiting. They had shrunk themselves and the furniture down to near-human size, another hospitable gesture, although my chair was still high enough that my feet dangled well above the smooth stone floor.

"You look much better," Nalan said as I sat back and warily scrutinized the feast that was spread out over the huge table. Nothing looked at all familiar.

"Thanks. I feel a lot better. What was that knock-out drink all about, anyway?" I asked as I picked up a dark red roll and began to slather it with something that looked like lavender-colored butter. It smelled a bit different from normal bread, but it still had that yeasty scent, so I felt comfortable trying it out first. "Were you guys putting some kind of spell on me?"

"Not at all!" Arala exclaimed. "That was just a relaxation tonic meant to open up your mind. We wanted to give you the knowledge you need to leave the Tua realm, but you were tense and tired. The tonic should have put you in a more receptive state of mind."

"Unfortunately, it turns out that it was too strong for your constitution," Nalan said. "Due to your shifter nature, it did no lasting harm, and simply put you to sleep. We will have to do this another way, but first, let us eat. As we understand, regular feeding is very important for your health."

I reluctantly agreed, worried at this evidence that they were not all-knowing and could make dangerous mistakes. Did I understand correctly that their tonic could have killed me if I'd been human? How safe was the breakfast spread, then? I decided to eat only small quantities of any one food and use Fenris's detection spells to ensure nothing was poisonous to me.

We spent the next hour talking over breakfast, or was it brunch? They might have entirely different mealtimes here than on my world, and it didn't seem important enough to ask.

Nalan and Arala explained that they were the last of their line, and that the forest I had been traveling in was only a tiny part of their domain. They were old enough to live on their own, though they were not yet adults by Tua standards—having lived for a mere eight hundred years of our time. That put them close to Iannis's age, I reflected, but they seemed to mature a lot more slowly.

I asked if the entire world was so sparsely populated as the bits I had seen, and they explained that there were a few small towns, but most of their world was wilderness. The Tua were not a particularly fertile race—they could only bear one child every five hundred years or so. Breeding with humans was far easier but frowned upon by Tua society. Even so, every once in a while, some adventurous Tua would take up with a mortal from the other realm. From their disapproving tone, it sounded like Ta's-radala had defied her own realm's customs as much as Recca's when she kidnapped Iannis's grandfather.

I listened intently to their words, aware that, as far as I knew, no other human had ever gotten a Tua to sit down and talk about their society like this. Iannis and Fenris would be thrilled at this information, if I ever got out of here. "We regret that we insulted you earlier by questioning your relationship with Iannis," Arala said as she polished off a leg of what seemed to be pheasant, if pheasant meat was deep blue. "While you were asleep, Nalan and I have been looking through and discussing your memories, and now we understand better why it is such a sensitive subject. As far as I am concerned, being part Tua, he seems a worthy partner for you."

I wanted to say that the Tua connection was the part I could do without, but that would have been a lie. I would not change a single thing about Iannis, not even the bits he got from Ta'sradala.

"He is so busy lately that you don't see enough of him," Nalan added with a pitying glance. "Politics in your world seem quite complicated, and unnecessarily so. Here in the Tua realm, we do not much regard shape or size or the type of power we wield, since everything can be changed so easily. Things would be much simpler in your world if you all treated each other as the same race."

"You should tell that to Ta'sradala," I said, unwillingly amused by Nalan's philosophic ruminations. "Some of us are pretty bigoted on Recca, I admit, but *her* sense of superiority is truly out of this world."

"Well, of course, she *is* Tua," Arala said, but stopped herself when she saw me bristle. "Oh, well, it's not likely we could ever agree on that. You don't know enough about us to have an accurate opinion."

"That's true, I guess, but I can't respect anyone who blatantly abuses their power," I said. "I guess there are good and bad Tua, just as there are good and bad mages or humans. But a bully is a bully."

As we continued the discussion, I was impressed by how quickly they grasped concepts and ideas based only on what they'd seen in my mind. Broghan was curled up on a bench nearby, and his eyes flicked back and forth between us attentively, as if he were following the whole conversation. I wondered if he understood everything that was being said.

"I am especially interested in meeting your absent friend, this Polar/Fenris individual," Alara said. "He is like you in some ways, Sunaya, and yet so very different, judging by his memories as compared to yours."

"Oh! Right," I said, remembering belatedly that they would have looked at Fenris's memories too. No wonder they'd been so fascinated—he'd seen much more of the world than I had, and was a scholar of magic and magical history. "Hopefully I'll get to see him again soon. I was so relieved when he called Iannis and confirmed that he was alive and well."

"I'm certain he'll return to you soon, no matter the danger," Nalan said confidently. "He cares for you and Iannis very much —he will not abandon you entirely."

After the meal, we continued our conversation with a walk on the grounds. Broghan accompanied us in eagle form, soaring overhead as the Tua led me through the gardens of their gigantic estate.

"I would like to learn more about this First Mage that your mages worship," Alara said as we walked along the edge of a shimmering purple pond. Giant red water lilies floated along the surface, and I caught a glimpse of multi-finned green fish swimming beneath the surface. "Fenris knew a lot about her teachings, but he had little information about her early life and origins. Does anyone know where she came from?"

"That's a better question for Fenris or Iannis," I said ruefully. "I'm still very new at being a mage and only learned about Resinah a year ago."

"Hmm," Nalan said, a distant but thoughtful expression on his face. "It seems that Fenris has heard about some memoirs written by her first disciples. Some of them have been lost forever, and others are kept locked up as sacred relics by their descendants. He has never been able to get at these records, though they are on his...bucket list, you call it?"

I suppressed a laugh—the Tua had expressed bafflement at Northian slang terms more than once. "A bucket list is a list of things that you want to accomplish before you die," I said. "Fenris is a scholar, so of course something like that would be on the list."

"What if Resinah was one of us?" Alara asked suddenly, her face brightening at the possibility. "She might very well have been amongst the first Tua to cross over to the human realm, and may have taken it upon herself to bring magic to your people."

"There seem to be reports that she was extraordinarily tall for a human," Nalan said. "Perhaps she adjusted her size to fit in better?"

"You mean like Ta'sradala did?" I asked. "She's tall, but nothing like you guys when I first saw you."

Nalan nodded. "She would be taller than even us in our realm, since she is much older. But we would frighten you if we walked through Recca in our natural forms, so it is only natural that we would shrink down to a more manageable size."

I snorted at that. Eight feet was still considered freakishly tall by anyone's standards, especially for a woman. But, admittedly, it wasn't unheard of, whereas a thirty-foot tall giant would definitely attract attention.

"I don't know about that theory," I said after I'd thought about it for a moment. "The mages believe that Resinah's power came directly from the Creator, and by all accounts, she wasn't the type of person to create a whole religion based on a lie." The mages back home would be outraged at the very suggestion. Could the same race have produced a Resinah *and* a Ta'sradala? They were like night and day.

Nalan shrugged a broad shoulder. "I don't see how it is a lie. Our own powers come from the Creator."

So they believed in the Creator, too. "Is Resinah a Tua name?" I asked.

"Well, no. And your magic language, Loranian, does not resemble ours at all. But she would have used an alias while on such a mission and made up an entirely new language," Nalan speculated. "That would be as easy as a child's game for any of us."

"It would be very out of character for a Tua to go live amongst humans and pose as one of them," Alara admitted. "But we too have our share of curious and eccentric individuals, and Resinah could have been one of them. If mages are descended from our race, it would explain why they have longer lifespans than ordinary humans. And why mages from Manuc, where we Tua most often visit, live so much longer than those in other countries."

"About that," I said warily, looking them up and down again. "Given your huge size, it is a bit surprising that you can have children with humans at all."

"Why?" Alara said. "We can take any form or size at will—just look at Broghan. We are able to breed with any race we run across, no matter how exotic—not that we would necessarily care to."

"Coming back to our original subject—the legend that the First Mage did not die, but merely vanished during an ocean voyage, implies that she may very well have returned to the Tua realm," Nalan said in a reasonable voice. "Or perhaps she has gone on to explore another world entirely."

I scowled. He spoke as if she was still alive, when the First Mage had died over four thousand years ago. "If that's the case, then why is it that she still responds to petitioners in her own temples?" I asked. "I've personally spoken to her on more than one occasion. If she's gone off to some other world, or back to the Tua realm, then how is it that she still hears and answers us?"

The Tua fell silent for a long moment. "You make a very good point," Alara finally said. "We shall have to investigate this further. Surely there are records that will tell us who went missing from the Tua realm within the relevant time period."

"Yes, I believe there are," Nalan concurred. "What a delightful little mystery you've given us, Sunaya! This will keep us busy for some time. And if we are right, then you are our very remote relative." He grinned down at me.

"I still don't know that your theory makes sense," I pointed out, not wanting them to get too attached to the possibility. "Only some mages are direct descendants of the First Mage anyway. Legend has it that she was able to transmit her mage power to the other disciples, which is how power was passed down through other family lines. Are the Tua able to do that?"

"Of course we can," Nalan said, sounding a bit miffed. "It is no trouble at all to gift a small measure of power to someone else—our own magic regenerates quickly enough, so it is no loss to us."

"Here," Alara said, pressing her index finger to the palm of my hand. "See for yourself."

I cried out as a sudden jolt of power hit me. My own magic reacted, and I felt power swell inside me like a river during springtime, until I was certain I was going to burst before it finally settled back down. Frowning, I examined it—my magic was at a much higher level, I realized with amazement. Could this be a permanent change?

"You say that's just a tiny part of your magic?" I asked faintly. Now that I was looking closer, I could see that Alara had doubled my magic with a mere touch of the hand. It was uncomfortably similar to how Resinah herself had passed power down to her disciples, if the stories could be believed.

"Yes," she said. "That was as much as you could safely absorb. I could try to give you more, but it would likely unmake your entire being."

"No, no, that's all right," I said. I swallowed hard as I looked up at her. No wonder the Tua were considered legendary—they were practically divine beings, especially compared to those who possessed no magic of their own.

"Are you all right?" Nalan said, gazing down at me with concern. "It occurs to me that your mind may have trouble grasping so much in such a short time."

"I'm fine," I said, waving away his concern. "And really, thank you for the gift." It was going to take me a while to get used to the new magic humming in my veins, and I wondered if I was nearly as strong as Iannis now. "Unfortunately, this gift isn't going to do me much good unless I can get out of here. You both are so extraordinarily powerful—isn't there a way you can send me back home, to Iannis?"

The Tua shook their heads sadly. "Unfortunately, our laws forbid us to interfere in the affairs of an older member of our race," Alara said.

"However," Nalan conceded, a thoughtful look on his face, "as we told you earlier, we can give you a bit of knowledge, to help even the playing field, as your race would say."

"I'll take anything I can get," I said fervently.

"We wish you good fortune," Alara said solemnly as she touched the nape of my neck again.

I felt that strange sensation of my mind parting again, but this time, instead of something being pulled out, there was immense pressure instead. I gasped as it drove me to my knees, and heard Broghan squawk in alarm as my vision went dark.

"Goodbye, young Sunaya," Nalan said, his voice sounding very far away. And then everything went black.

———

WHEN I OPENED my eyes again, I found myself kneeling in the same forest where I'd first entered the Tua realm. Disoriented, I got to my feet, then took stock of myself to make sure that everything was in order. I was still wearing the leathers Arala and Nalan had given me, and to my delight, they'd replenished the food and water stores in my magical sleeve. Strangely, there was a snakeskin belt with a pretty copper buckle wrapped around my waist that I was fairly certain I hadn't been wearing before. It was cool to the touch, and as I skimmed my fingers across the black and bronze scales, I wondered if there was anything magical about it.

Putting that question aside for now, I set up a ward around the perimeter of the clearing, then sat down and warily began to sift through my mind for the knowledge that the Tua had promised me. Sure enough, I found it, appearing in my mind's eye like a beautifully fashioned trunk that needed to be unpacked. Carefully, I mentally turned the copper key and unclasped the latch, then lifted the lid.

Unlike Fenris's knowledge transfer, this trunk contained no personal memories, just a treasure trove of useful information, like a whole lifetime of textbooks, encyclopedias, and dictionaries in one heap. I gasped as it rushed into me all at once, struggling not to go under in the tide of strange ideas and knowledge, and quickly erected a mental barrier to channel this new influx safely. I imagined a library inside my mind, like Janta's back in Solantha, and that is where I directed the new knowledge, ready to be consulted when needed.

Suddenly, I understood the nature of the different dimensions. There was an infinity of them aside from Recca and the Tua realm, both dangerous and wondrous in their own ways. Despite their differences, some dimensions were contiguous, like squares of fabric stitched together into one giant quilt. It was possible to get from one to the other, though only a handful were easily accessible from any specific location, and some shifted erratically. Recca and the Tua realm were close neighbors, as dimensions went. The Tua had left the instructions for how to return from their dimension to Recca right in my head. The spell was based on some complicated mathematics, but since the dimensions were currently in close conjunction, simply speaking it would be enough for now.

The problem was, the transfer required a Tua-sized expenditure of magic. Would I be able to perform the spell on my own? With the extra boost in power they had given me, I might just be able to swing it, though from what I understood there was at least an even chance I wouldn't make it.

Excitement and fear coursed through me all at once, and I wiped my suddenly damp palms on my hands. If I could make this work, I would make it back to Recca, and there would only be one more test to go. But if I failed...I would end up in the void, and die of asphyxiation.

Closing my eyes, I sent up a short but fervent prayer to Magorah to watch over me and make sure that my magic did not falter. Gathering my power, I clasped my hands together, then spoke the spell in the strange language of the Tua, which I now knew as well as Northian, thanks to Nalan and Alara.

As soon as I spoke the Words, the magic inside me was sucked away, leaving me weak and empty. I gasped as a sonic boom rendered me nearly deaf, and the next thing I knew, the world was spinning away from me. Pressure squeezed all around me until I was nearly certain that I'd been flattened into a pancake, and I clasped my hands to the sides of my head, trying to alleviate the pain and the ringing sound in my ears.

Everything around me went black, and there was no air, no sound, no light. I gasped soundlessly for air as horror froze my blood, realizing that I was in the void. I'd fucked up. I was going to die out here, and Iannis would never see me again. He wouldn't even be able to recover my dead body...

But just as my limbs were starting to go numb, I felt a sudden push from behind, and I slammed into a giant glowing ball of light that appeared out of nowhere. I crashed into the ground on my hands and knees, panting hard, my fingers curling around fistfuls of dirt and grass. The meal I'd enjoyed with the Tua earlier came barreling straight up my throat, and I puked for what felt like endless minutes, heaving my guts up until there was absolutely nothing left.

Finally, when the puking had turned to dry heaving, I flopped onto my back as far from the mess as I could manage. My limbs had turned to water, and everything *hurt*. But my heart was still beating strong in my chest, and my senses still worked. I could smell the sweet grass and flowers of Ennartha's garden, could feel the cool wind and tiny drops of moisture on my face. An echo of Ta'sradala's scent made my stomach clench, but at least she wasn't nearby just now to witness my abject humiliation.

Who had given me the push that saved my life? I'd probably never know, but whatever the cause, I had made it back to Recca. Perhaps not to Solantha, where I most wanted to go, but at least I had arrived back in my own world. And I was in one piece.

13

I rested in the garden for a good twenty minutes before I finally found the strength to move. Once the dizziness and nausea had subsided, I fished a piece of stale bread from my magical sleeve and gnawed on it to settle my upset stomach. The bit of food helped, and I struggled to my feet so I could get my bearings.

As I'd surmised from the scents, I was in Ennartha's garden again. The position of the sun told me it was mid-day, and it was still high summer judging by the fact that the same flowers were still growing and the weather hadn't changed. But was it the same year that I'd left? How much time had I lost?

One thing at a time, Sunaya, I told myself. At least I *had* made it back. From what I could tell, there was nobody around—surely my arrival would have drawn attention if anybody was home. Even if I'd made no sound, any competent mage, let alone a Tua like Ta'sradala, would have sensed the powerful magic I'd used for the dimensional transfer. Most likely they hadn't expected me to survive and come back at all, and had all gone off to do something else.

As I absently plucked some blackberries from a bush and popped them into my mouth, I had to admit I was feeling more confident despite the uncertainty of my circumstances. I had a much better sense of appreciation for Ta'sradala's power now that I'd had a glimpse of the Tua realm, but I was also armed with knowledge of my own that might help me. I sure as hell wouldn't be telling Ta'sradala or her daughter about what I'd learned—I had a feeling that would have dire consequences, both for me and the Tua who'd helped me get back here.

I briefly considered leaving Ennartha's place altogether and trying to make my way to Iannis alone, but I worried that he might arrive while I was gone. The serapha charm was still not working, so there was no way to tell. Besides, Ta'sradala could snatch me up at any time, from any place, and even with my increased power, there was nothing I could do about that. Her magic seemed to operate on a different frequency than my own —I would need to learn to use Tua spells in order to combat her, but with the huge disparity in power, it wouldn't make much difference.

Thinking about it, it seemed strange that Ta'sradala's magic would be different from my own, if the theory about Resinah being a Tua was true. Shouldn't our spells be the same? But perhaps our magic had evolved into something different over the millennia, something inferior to the original.

Half-heartedly, I pulled the gulaya from my sleeve and attempted to recharge it with my new powers. Unfortunately, the extra magic was of no use— I still needed to perform that tiresome recharging ritual, and I didn't have the right ingredients necessary for the spell.

Wandering the gardens, I found Drawe sitting on a secluded bench, reading a book. He was still dressed in simple, drab clothing, but his hair was washed and he was clean, with no signs that he'd recently performed any labor.

Definitely not a servant.

"Hey," I said softly, moving a little closer. I angled my head to try and see the title of the book he was reading—a compendium of Manucan folk tales. "How's it going?"

The boy jumped, his blue eyes widening at the sight of me. "You shouldn't be here," he whispered, looking around. "You should flee before *she* comes back!"

I had no doubt by the tone of his voice which "she" he was referring to, and part of me wanted to do just that. But I had questions that needed answering. "You look similar to Iannis, my husband-to-be," I said, keeping my voice low. "Are you related?"

"I guess so," Drawe said. "Nana Deryna is my great-grandmother, and Iannis's aunt."

I nodded—it made much more sense than that old woman being his mother. "Why don't you live with your parents?"

"They died when I was a baby," Drawe said sadly. "Nana says

they got mixed up with an angry Tua. I'd never met one before... before recently..." he added, his eyes darting around again. "She frightens me."

"The Tua frighten me too," I said solemnly, feeling sorry for the boy. No wonder he was so quiet—he was forced to be around a living nightmare! "But they are not all bad. I just came back from the Tua realm, and the two I came across were quite nice. They helped me get back here."

Drawe looked at me like I was nuts. "There is no way you went to the Tua realm," he protested. "No human who has ever gone there has come back on their own, at least not for hundreds of years. Nana said it is deadly for humans."

I shrugged. "I'm not human. Maybe that helps."

Drawe still looked skeptical, and I decided to drop the subject. "If you're unhappy here, you can always come back to Canalo with me," I said. "There are a few other children around your age who live in the palace, and I think you'd get along with them quite well."

Drawe scowled. "That's never going to happen. *She* is never going to let that happen. Don't you get it? That old Tua lady is doing everything she can to make sure your wedding won't happen and that you won't ever go home. I didn't expect you to survive this long, but it's only a question of time. She's playing a game of cat and mouse, and *you're* the mouse."

I opened my mouth to respond indignantly to that—I was a *panther*, not some damned mouse!—when I felt a sizzle of magic in the air, coming from the side of the house. Drawe gasped, then scurried off to hide just as Ta'sradala came storming toward us. She was furious, her eyes blazing with cold anger, her lips pressed in a thin line. The air around her shimmered with waves of power.

But I wasn't afraid. Not this time.

"I could be wrong," I said casually, turning to face her, "but it seems like you're unhappy to see me."

"How did you get back?" she demanded, stopping a few feet away from me. "You should not have been able to. Mortals cannot travel between planes."

I shrugged. "I have my resources."

Her eyes narrowed as she looked me up and down. "You look healthy," she accused. "Like you've slept and eaten. You're even wearing new clothes."

My lips tugged into a smirk. "Like I said. Resources." I wasn't about to give up the names of the Tua who had helped me—for all I knew that could get them into trouble, and that was the last thing I wanted. "Are we done here yet? I've already proved I'm more than capable of passing your tests. I hope I haven't missed my own wedding yet, or there will be hell to pay when Iannis finds me."

"You still have one more test," Ta'sradala said, her lips curving into a cruel smirk of her own. "Let's see if your 'resources' can help you with *this*, mortal."

She waved her hand, and I braced myself as the world began to spin around me once more. I squeezed my eyes shut to keep the nausea at bay, thankful that I'd already vomited everything in my stomach. Whatever she threw at me, I vowed to myself, I would not give up. I had to get back to Iannis one way or the other, and the hope of seeing him again would have to give me the endurance I needed to survive.

14

When I next opened my eyes, I found myself standing in what looked to be an underground cave. Glowing mushrooms covered the walls, illuminating the interior just enough to make out the silhouettes of bats hanging overhead and the glimmer of a deathly still lake below. A shiver crawled down my spine as I craned my neck, trying to see how far the tunnel up ahead went, but the glow from the mushrooms was too dim to be of much help at that distance. Just how far underground was I? And in what world?

Parched, I made my way over to the lake, and after checking it for harmful substances, sipped the water to wash out the last taste of vomit from my dry mouth. It was ice cold, but tasted divine, and I quickly gulped down several handfuls. My canteen was still full of water, so I didn't refill it, but with any luck there would be more water sources down here should I run out.

Thirst quenched, I sat down a few feet away from the lake, then treated myself to a little picnic. I was still a bit dizzy, so I ate slowly, replenishing my strength with the food the Tua had given me. I was getting used to the strange tastes and was so hungry that it wouldn't have mattered if they'd given me week-old gruel.

As I polished off a leg of blue roast bird, something shifted around my waist. Looking down, I shrieked—the belt I'd been wearing earlier had turned into a living snake! I jumped up, conjuring a fireball in my hands, but before I could incinerate the beast, it morphed into a wolf cub.

"Broghan!" I gasped, extinguishing the flame. I hadn't realized that Nalan and Alara's pet could change into inanimate objects. Would I ever cease to be surprised by Tua magic? And why was he here?

"Can I have some food?" he asked me in mindspeak, and I stared. His voice was that of a young boy. *"I haven't eaten anything since we left the Tua realm."*

"Sure," I said warily, sitting back down. I offered him some of the meat and bread, which he wolfed down eagerly—pardon the pun. "You've been able to speak this whole time?"

"Yes, but there was no need to," he said. *"Nalan and Alara were doing fine answering your questions."*

I snorted at that. "Do they know you're here?"

Broghan said nothing, curling up at my feet and rubbing his cold nose against my leg. I scratched the back of his ears, still feeling a bit disconcerted.

"Broghan," I said again, a little more firmly. "Does *anyone* know you're here?"

"I wanted to see the human world for myself." He sounded a little petulant now. *"Without waiting forever for the others to make up their minds. Nalan and Alara would never have let me go if I'd told them, so I hitched a ride with you. And it's a good thing I did, since you got stuck."*

I gasped. "Was it you who pushed me the last bit of the way?"

"Duh."

Well, that was one mystery solved. A talking Tua pet possessed more power than me, even with my original strength doubled. And had saved my hide. It was more than a little humbling.

"Thank you," I said, a bit stiffly. "But the last thing I need is for the Tua to think I stole you away."

Broghan licked my hand. *"You won't get in trouble for this,"* he assured me. *"I'll make sure of it."*

I wasn't so sure about *that*, but it wasn't as if I could just banish him. He would probably come right back, and it was a waste of magic, anyway. "I am glad you're here with me," I admitted as I stroked his furry back. "It's nice to have company in this gloomy place."

We finished our picnic, and then Broghan morphed into an otter and plunged into the lake. I'd always been perfectly happy with my shifter form, but now that I'd met him, I was a little envious that he seemed to be able to change into whatever he wanted.

As Broghan splashed about in the water, I focused on my serapha charm, trying to sense Iannis. As before, there was no trace of him. I was certain that Ta'sradala had done something to disrupt the charm—there was no way he was dead. He'd been safe and sound at the palace when I'd left. Surely he was on his way over here by now, wasn't he? Iannis was one of the most intelligent men I'd ever met—he would have figured out where I'd gone by this point. How much time had passed since I'd left? A week? By Magorah, the girls were probably worried sick. I felt bad for disappearing on them like that, but it wasn't as if I'd had a choice. I hoped they were doing okay.

"Come on, Broghan," I called as I headed toward the tunnel up ahead. "Let's see where this thing goes."

The challenge, I surmised as Broghan caught up with me, morphing into a giant bat, was to figure out how to get out of this blasted place. The bats, which had been hanging peacefully before, had awakened at my presence, and were flitting overhead in weird patterns. I conjured a glow light to help with illumination as we walked, but as we moved from cave to cave, there was nothing but endless caverns. This underground world was beautiful in its own way, full of glowing plants and wonderful rock formations, but aside from the bats, there was little to eat down here. I needed to find a way out before I ran out of food.

Broghan, for his part, seemed to be having the time of his life. He chased some of the other bats around the caverns and did somersaults and a few other aerial tricks. I told him to stay close to me so he wouldn't get lost, but he only laughed. He probably couldn't get lost if he tried, and found it amusing that I was trying to look out for his welfare.

Wondering if I could make the bats work for me, I picked up some pebbles and tossed them at the bats, noting which direction they fled. Several of them darted for one tunnel in particular, and I followed, hoping it led to the surface instead of deeper into the cave. I repeated the process a few more times, but eventually it became harder, as the bats would disappear through holes in the cave ceiling too high for me to reach. I tried to follow them with the levitation spell, but the bats were too fast. Some of them vanished through a confusing field of sharp and spiny stalactites that hung so close together they formed a lattice. I had to find a way around.

Eventually, I dropped back down to the ground again. Even though I was much stronger now, constant use of the levitation spell would deplete my magic eventually. There was enough illumination here from the glowing mushrooms that I extinguished my glow light. Broghan shrank into a normal-sized bat, albeit one with bright red fur, and landed on my shoulder.

"Tired of flying?" I asked as he leaned his warm, tiny body against my neck. Rather than answer, he licked my earlobe, and I couldn't help giggling. Regardless of the consequences, I was really glad he had come along. Having a companion kept me grounded, which was more important than ever since I couldn't feel Iannis anymore. I had not realized how comforting the tiny speck of his essence in the necklace had been until it went silent. One more crime to hold against his cursed grandmother.

Using the dim greenish light from the mushrooms, I tried to

follow the bats' trail from the ground. But the floor in this stretch of the cave system was brittle and uneven, and it was slow going as I picked a path between the various clusters of stalagmites. Some of them were taller than me, and I felt like I was walking through a forest of stone, while others were tiny, like thick blades of grass, and I had to skirt around them to avoid cutting myself on their sharp edges.

I'd just spied another tunnel up ahead when my foot slipped on some loose pebbles. "Whoa!" I cried as I slid down a steep slope. Conjuring a light, my heart leapt into my throat as I shot straight into a wide, bottomless fissure. I dropped a good thirty feet before I managed to activate the levitation spell, but I was falling too fast by then for it to fight gravity. A scream tore from my throat as I continued to plummet, and I frantically searched Fenris's spell catalogue, trying to find something, anything that could help me before I crashed into the rocks below...

Strong claws clamped around my arms, and I looked up to see Broghan flapping his wings above me, a giant eagle now. He soared out of the fissure and deposited me safely on the other side. I collapsed, my body shaking from delayed reaction, and I laid my head on the cool ground, panting with fear and relief.

"Thank you," I choked out when I finally had enough breath to speak. "I thought I was a goner."

Broghan nuzzled my face—he was back in wolf cub form again. *"Watch where you're stepping,"* he said. *"You gave me a scare."*

I laughed. "Gave *you* a scare?" I asked, rubbing the top of his head. He curled up against me, and we lay there for a long moment, until my legs had stopped shaking and I was ready to move on again.

We spent the next couple of hours climbing up and down through the caves, until my stomach was gnawing at me with hunger and my limbs were beginning to ache with exhaustion. It had been a long time since I'd done this much physical activity, and I'd been growing out of shape to begin with. Too many parties and meetings, and not enough sparring with Rylan—I'd make sure to keep up my form, if I ever got out of here.

When I got out of here, I corrected myself. I couldn't accept anything less.

We paused for another short break to tuck into the last of the provisions, and between the two of us, we polished them off pretty quickly. Eventually, we came upon another underground lake, where I gratefully refilled my now-empty canteen. As I drank directly from the lake, I spotted some eyeless, pinkish salamanders as big as eels swimming in the water. Using a spell Iannis had taught me on our last vacation, I snagged one from the lake, then flash-roasted it. Broghan wrinkled his nose at the smell, and turned up his nose when I offered him a bite, but I devoured the whole thing. It tasted a bit sour, but the texture and color were similar to shrimp. I closed my eyes and tried to imagine I was in the palace, enjoying a seafood dinner with Iannis.

Hopefully I could do that soon, if I ever found a way out of these blasted caves.

———

WE HIKED through the caves for several more hours before I grew too exhausted to continue, then made camp in a relatively flat and dry spot. There were no twigs or branches around to light a fire with, but Broghan changed into a bear, and I curled into his furry bulk as I slept. His big, warm body was a welcome contrast to the frigid stone floor of the cavern, and I was able to catch a few hours of sleep before we continued on.

"Is that a light?" Broghan asked as we trudged through yet another stalagmite-filled cavern. Looking up, I saw him flit into one of the three tunnels up ahead. *"Yes, I think we're almost there!"*

The excitement in Broghan's voice sent a surge of energy through me, and I jogged to catch up with him in the tunnel. We came through the other side into a much smaller cavern, and sure enough, a ray of light speared through the endless darkness. Following it, I saw that it came from a hole in the wall a good forty feet up. From the light coming through, it had to be daytime.

"Dammit," I said as I levitated up there to examine the hole. "This is way too small." I stuck my arm through the hole, and the sensation of wind caressing my fingers encouraged me further. "We have to figure out how to enlarge it."

My magic was starting to run low, so instead of using a spell, I found a sharp rock on the cavern floor and began chipping away. However, without standing on anything but air, I didn't have much leverage, so it was slow going. Luckily, the hole was being obstructed by encrusted bat dung and dirt rather than actual stone, or I would have been forced to use my magic to melt it away. Broghan turned into a dragon, then flew up to join me, using his sharp, steel-like claws to help me carve out the hole.

Finally, the opening was big enough for me to fit through, and I got onto my belly and wriggled out through the other side. But my relief was short-lived—the window we had opened was on the sheer, vertical side of a mountain. Terror gripped my throat as I stared at the verdant valleys far below—if I shimmied forward more than another foot or so, I would fall straight down and split my skull open on the rocky ground. And the winds here were far too high and unpredictable to risk the levitation spell.

"Hang on," Broghan said as he crawled through the hole behind me. He launched himself into the air, and with a few flaps of his wings propelled himself upward, beyond my field of vision. I considered twisting around to see where he was going, but I didn't want to accidentally fall off, so I waited anxiously.

A few moments later, Broghan soared back down, his dragon form ten times bigger than before. I ducked as his powerful wings blasted me in the face, and a small rock glanced off the back of my head.

"Climb on, quick!" Broghan ordered as I lifted my head. He pressed his body close enough to the mountainside that I could easily leap onto his back. But I was afraid that the blustery winds would carry me away before I landed, so instead I crawled carefully, gripping the tough membranes of his wings as I dragged myself across his big body. Several long, agonizing seconds later, I reached the depression between his wings and

collapsed there, breathing hard from fear and exertion. I wasn't usually afraid of heights, but it was a *long* way down from here.

Satisfied that I was properly mounted, Broghan launched himself from the face of the mountainside. I screamed, grabbing onto the spines jutting from his back as we plummeted straight for the valley below. We were in free fall for nearly a minute, and then he snapped out his wings and began to glide.

"You're going to give me a heart attack," I scolded as we coasted easily along the wind currents.

"Don't be so dramatic," Broghan chided. *"You're stronger than that. Where's your sense of adventure?"*

Where indeed? I thought as we landed in the middle of a large field. His antics made me feel positively sedate and middle-aged in comparison, even if they had saved my life several times now.

A herd of deer had been grazing nearby, but they all fled when Broghan's shadow covered the land. Thankfully there were no humans nearby to frighten—the last thing we needed was to draw attention to ourselves.

As I slid down from Broghan's back, I marveled at how quickly my life had changed yet again. Just last week, I'd been wishing I could get away from the palace and all the duties that had come along with it. Well, I'd gotten that wish, and had spent the last couple of days living experiences I'd never imagined in my wildest dreams. Or rather, nightmares.

I'd take paperwork and committee meetings over dealing with Ta'sradala any day, I admitted to myself as I sat down in the grass. At least back home Iannis had been close by, and I'd seen him every night, tired or not. I missed him so badly, it felt like one of my limbs had been severed, leaving me with a phantom ache I couldn't cure.

Broghan morphed back into the wolf cub and curled up next to me, as if he were trying to console me. He said nothing, simply being there for me as a warm and solid presence, and I was grateful for his company.

As we rested, I tried to muster some optimism. We'd made it out alive, and this had been the third and final test, hadn't it? Against all odds, I'd survived all her challenges. If she stood by her word, Ta'sradala had no choice but to let me return home to Iannis.

Would she, though? Ta'sradala couldn't be trusted to let me enjoy my victory; she might easily find some pretext to prolong this evil game of hers. People who accused others of cheating were most likely to do so themselves whenever it suited their purposes. A haughty Tua could be just as hypocritical as humans. And who would dare call her on her bullshit, anyway? Definitely not Iannis's mother, who didn't seem to have enough spine to stand up to Ta'sradala even if she wanted to. Anyway, I just wished she'd hurry up and spirit me back home. The sun was setting on yet another day, and I was running out of time.

15

At some point, I dozed off in the middle of the field, with Broghan using my chest as a pillow. I'd scrutinized the constellations above us earlier to try and determine if I was in Recca, but I hadn't been able to come up with a definitive answer, so I decided I might as well try to regain my strength. I was just having a nice dream about being back at home, surrounded by Iannis and my friends at a feast and sinking my teeth into a juicy haunch of meat, when I felt myself suddenly yanked away.

Opening my eyes, I found myself prone in Ennartha's garden once again, with the three women staring down at me. Deryna seemed relieved to see me and gave me a tentative smile. Ennartha was impassive, and Ta'sradala furious. I jumped to my feet, adrenaline rushing through my body as I realized I was finally back.

"I passed your tests," I said, jabbing a finger at Ta'sradala. "You have to take me back home now!"

"Hmph," Ta'sradala said. "I don't know about that. The only reason you survived was because of that silly shape-shifter who helped you out. Who was he, anyway? I didn't know any creatures like that lived in those caves."

I froze, looking around. Broghan wasn't anywhere nearby, and the snakeskin belt he'd previously disguised himself as was gone. *"Broghan?"* I called in mindspeak, a little anxious. *"Are you okay?"*

There was no reply.

What had happened to him? I guessed that when Ta'sradala had transported me back, Broghan had not come with me, since he wasn't attached to my body like he'd been last time. He was probably still in that field, poor thing. I hoped he would be all right on his own, though from recent experience, he seemed quite capable of taking care of himself.

"You never specified that I couldn't use outside help," I said tersely. "I've won your game fair and square. Now take me back."

"And why should I listen to an impertinent mortal like you?" Ta'sradala asked, looking down her nose at me. "You do not make demands of a Tua—you get on your knees and beg." The malicious glitter in her eyes told me even that would be no use —she would enjoy my humiliation without yielding an inch.

"I shouldn't even have to ask!" I thundered, losing my temper completely. "You told me that if I won, you would let me go, and I *have*! How are you any better than us 'mortals' if you can't be bothered to keep your own word?"

"She has a point, Mother," Ennartha said uneasily. "Surprising as it may be, she has completed the challenges."

"That is for *me* to decide!" Ta'sradala exclaimed angrily. "Besides, promises to humans don't count. Are you actually taking this pitiful mortal's side?"

"You are the *worst* person I have ever met," I hissed, my entire body vibrating with anger. I wanted to claw Ta'sradala's perfect face off, and indeed I might have thrown a punch or two if I didn't value my life. "I used to think that mages were the worst, but you are even more arrogant than they are, and faithless to boot."

I had to wonder if the mages got that side of their personality from the Tua, if Nalan and Alara's theory was correct. Or maybe power just naturally corrupted people and gave them that false sense of superiority. There were plenty of humans who were just as insufferable. At least Iannis was nothing like this crazy bitch. I felt a strong wave of longing, wishing he was here by my side.

"How dare you!" The Tua drew herself upright, and I braced myself for another magical attack.

"Go ahead," I taunted. "Choke me or burn me or send me into another dimension. That's what you always do when you're at a loss, isn't it? You can't bear to confront me so you throw your power around like the big bully you are."

Ta'sradala froze. "Please," Deryna begged, filling the shocked silence. "Our guest is speaking out of despair at being hopelessly outmatched, and she has just been through several exhausting, dangerous ordeals! Don't regard her words—her nerves must be shot. Consider the consequences before you do anything else, Ta'sradala. If Iannis finds out that you have hurt his beloved, or worse, he will never forgive any of us."

"I don't need my grandson's forgiveness," Ta'sradala said coldly, but she lowered her hand. "This mortal may be stronger and luckier than I'd been led to believe, but her impertinence is unforgiveable. We cannot allow such an undesirable trait to be grafted onto the family tree."

"Still," Ennartha said, and I blinked in surprise to see her speak up, "we should not be too hasty. Perhaps we should wait for Iannis to arrive and explain himself. We might yet convince him to desist from this match."

I shot her a glare—*thanks for that.* I was never going to like my future mother-in-law, but now she'd destroyed any chance of us getting along.

"He is surely going to arrive any day now," Deryna added, "and will be furious if his bride is not here."

"On the other hand"—Ennartha pursed her lips—"since he has not turned up yet, perhaps he is already thinking better of the connection and is too busy with his politics to chase after this girl. For all we know, the wedding may already be called off."

Fat chance, I thought contemptuously. She did not know Iannis at all if she really believed that.

"Besides," Deryna said, frowning thoughtfully, "didn't you tell us once that the Tua realm is forbidden to humans—and shifters, we must suppose—without special permission of the High

King? I understand he was not pleased when Ennartha took Iannis there all those years ago. Did you get permission before sending Sunaya there?"

Ta'sradala's shoulders stiffened, and for the first time, an uneasy look crossed her face. "Did you meet anyone while you were in the Tua realm, girl?" she asked sharply. "Or take anything that was not freely given?"

I scowled, refusing to answer. I did not want to get Nalan and Arala into trouble, and I knew that Broghan wasn't supposed to have come with me. If I told her that he had followed me from the Tua realm, I could land myself in even more trouble than I was in now.

"I'm getting tired of all these questions," I said, turning away. "If you aren't going to send me home, then I'll find a way back myself." I was perfectly capable of walking to the nearest village or town and securing transport of some kind. With any luck, there might even be an apothecary that sold the ingredients I needed to recharge my gulaya.

"I don't think so," Ta'sradala snapped. Magic sizzled around me, and my arms and legs snapped taut against my body, rendering me immobile. "You'll be staying right here until I figure out what to do with you."

———

I'D BEEN WORRIED that Ta'sradala would leave me out in the garden, frozen like a statue, but instead she locked me up in one of the bedrooms, which in a way was even worse. As I lay there on the bed, unable to so much as blink, my mind raced. I furiously tried to figure out how to escape this latest predicament. There were all sorts of spells that could undo immobilization, but, as before, my magic didn't work on the Tua's. She was simply too powerful, her magic too different for mine to work against hers.

At least I can breathe, I thought miserably as I stared up at the ceiling. My bodily functions were working just fine, as evidenced by my near bursting bladder. I needed to pee so badly I thought I might die, but I couldn't even wet the bed, I was frozen so stiff. I sincerely hoped that Ta'sradala wasn't going to force me to do any more tests. For all I knew she could be planning to put me through an endless series of challenges, claiming I had been cheating every time I won, until my strength and ingenuity finally gave out and I died.

Tears stung at my eyes as another wave of helplessness overcame me, and a scream built in my chest that I couldn't release no matter how hard I tried. What had I done to deserve this torture? Was I destined to be Ta'sradala's plaything for the rest of my life, simply because I'd dared to love her grandson? Was I going to die before I ever saw Iannis again?

And yet...even knowing what I knew now, I still wouldn't have changed a thing. I hadn't thought so at the time, but being taken prisoner by Iannis was the best thing that had ever happened to me. I had learned so much about myself, and had grown far more powerful and confident than I ever would have if I'd simply kept my head down and lived out my existence as an enforcer. Beneath his stern exterior, Iannis was wise and compassionate, with a heart of gold that so few people got to touch.

I was extraordinarily lucky to be one of those few.

As the hours passed with excruciating slowness, I tried to call for Broghan again. But if he was anywhere nearby, he didn't answer. Wouldn't he have caught up with me by now? Or was he stuck back in the cave world? Maybe he was afraid of Ta'sradala, too. Or, for all I knew, something else had caught his attention and he was off on another adventure. Broghan was fun-loving and capricious, and he didn't seem to have any concept of danger. I had a feeling he was just as likely to come after me as he was to befriend someone else and go off looking for trouble.

Finally, just when I thought I could bear no more of this, the door opened. "Apologies for keeping you waiting so long," Deryna murmured as she came inside with a tray of food. I felt a jolt of surprise at the sight of Ennartha right behind her, and I would have fallen off the bed if I'd been able to move.

"If Mother gets angry, this is on you," Ennartha said to Deryna, not looking at all happy as she waved her hand to unlock the spell. I groaned in relief as my muscles finally relaxed. Sitting up, I winced as aches and pains rippled through me—everything was stiff from being locked up for so long. "I was never here," Ennartha added with a warning glance at both of us as she left the room.

Deryna sat the tray next to me on the bed and took a seat, but I shook my head and rolled off to the other side. I was hungry, but my bladder was going to explode if I didn't use the facilities. I hobbled off to relieve myself, then came back to find that Deryna was still waiting for me.

"Why are you helping me?" I asked as I slowly sat down on the edge of the bed. A bowl of hot stew and thick slices of soda bread were waiting, and my mouth watered as I lifted the tray onto my lap.

"Because I don't think it's right, what Ta'sradala is doing," Deryna said. "I wish I could do more, but she is far too powerful for me to stand against, and as you can see, my sister is not inclined to intervene."

"No kidding," I said after I'd swallowed a spoonful of stew. "If Ennartha is your sister, does that make you half-Tua as well?" I didn't understand why she looked so old, if that was the case.

Deryna shook her head. "We are half-sisters," she explained. "I was born from our father's real wife, long after Ennartha was brought to us. We had other siblings, too, but I'm the only one left alive. It is frustrating," she added, her wrinkled features tightening into a scowl, "to be powerless in one's own house."

I stared. "You mean to say that this estate belongs to you?"

She nodded. "Ennartha does not stay in one place very long—she travels extensively. Since she is family, I have allowed her to keep a residence here, but the estate is legally mine." She sighed. "I am especially concerned about the effect Ta'sradala's visit is having on my great-grandson. He lost his family to the Tua and is scared to death of her."

I nodded sympathetically. "He told me about that earlier," I said.

"I invited him to stay with Iannis and me in Canalo. When this is all over, you should bring him there. Iannis said that Ta'sradala is unlikely to ever go to the Federation."

Deryna opened her mouth to answer, then stopped as we heard a loud commotion downstairs.

"Where is Sunaya?" Iannis thundered, his fury echoing through the entire house. "She had better be here, safe and unharmed, Mother, or there will be hell to pay!"

16

"By the Lady," Deryna exclaimed, rising from her chair. "Is that Iannis?"

I hopped off the bed as excitement rushed through my veins, eager to bound down the stairs and straight into his arms. But my legs were still stiff, so I was forced to hobble. Not exactly the way I'd imagined reuniting with Iannis, but it sure as hell beat never seeing him again.

"I'm surprised it took you so long to get here," Ta'sradala said in a silky voice, and I froze. She was already back? My heart sank. "I knew that mortal was bad news, Iannis. She's made you weaker."

"Nonsense," Iannis said. "I simply hadn't expected you to hide out in Aunt Deryna's house like a criminal."

"How dare you speak to your grandmother that way!" Ennartha scolded. "You were taught to respect your elders and show better manners than that."

"I would not call my manners to account if I were you just now, Mother," Iannis said icily. "You have both gone far beyond the pale, kidnapping my bride-to-be. You even blocked our seraphA charms so we could not sense each other. How could you connive at such cruelty?"

"It ill becomes you to storm and shout like this, Iannis," Ta's-radala said sharply. "You are behaving like a human—no, worse, like that hybrid brat you've foolishly decided to marry. Clearly, she has exerted a very bad influence on you. I don't know why you're so angry—girls come and go, and marriage is really not a good idea for people as long-lived as us. If you wish to start a family, I know a Tua female with a fascination for exotics like yourself." I could practically hear the feline smile in her voice. "She would give you a strong, long-lived child. This feeble, short-lived mortal is simply not a proper match for you."

Iannis said something, but I didn't hear it, because my ears were roaring and I was seeing red. Ignoring my stiff legs, I jumped down the rest of the steps, then burst into the sitting room.

"I've had enough of you," I spat as Ta'sradala and Ennartha stared at me, startled. "Iannis and I are getting married whether you like it or not, and there is absolutely *nothing* you can do about it."

"Sunaya!" As he spun toward me, the anger melted from Iannis's face, replaced with relief. I leapt into his arms, and he crushed me tightly against him. Joy swept through me as I kissed him fiercely, clutching at his broad shoulders as I inhaled his familiar scent. The stress and misery that had plagued me evaporated, leaving me feeling safe and warm in his arms.

"Are you all right?" Iannis asked in mindspeak, his mouth still pressed against mine. Tears stung my eyes at the concern in his voice, but I blinked them back—I would sooner die than dissolve into tears in front of his grandmother.

"I'm fine," I assured him, not wanting to rile him up with everything that had happened just yet. *"I'm just glad you're finally here."*

"I'm sorry it took so long for me to arrive," Iannis said ruefully. *"I did not have a gulaya keyed to Manuc, and it took me some time to figure out exactly where you were, never mind the travel time to get here. Not to mention a hurricane blew the ship off course."*

"How long has it been since I disappeared?"

"Twelve days."

"Please tell me that it isn't going to take that long to get back." That was cutting it *way* too close to the wedding date.

"Of course not. I've brought a gulaya. We'll be returning home shortly."

"Make sure not to use it in front of your grandmother. I tried that, and she disarmed mine before I could activate it."

"If you two are quite finished with this disgustingly sentimental display," Ta'sradala said coldly, "I don't believe we are done with this conversation."

"We most certainly are," Iannis said as we reluctantly broke apart. "Sunaya and I are going home now."

"Iannis," Deryna said soothingly, having come in at some point while we were embracing. "I understand that you are angry, and rightfully so. But it has been an age since you have come to visit. Please, at least sit down for a meal with us before you go, like a real family."

"A real family?" Iannis said, his voice tight with barely leashed rage. "Is this the sort of behavior a 'real family' engages in?"

Ta'sradala snorted contemptuously and vanished from sight. Was she truly gone, or simply invisible? Everyone else seemed to relax, so hopefully the former. She'd be back soon enough, I guessed, as leaving the rest of us in peace was hardly on her agenda. Or was she finally conceding defeat and allowing us to return to Canalo?

"I am truly sorry for what your bride has endured," Deryna said to Iannis. "Please know I had no part in it—you know how we cannot stand up to your grandmother, no matter how outrageous she becomes. But there is a family member you have not yet met." She pulled her skirts to the left, revealing Drawe, who had been hiding behind her. "This is Drawe, your nephew."

Iannis's eyes widened in surprise. "Nephew?" he asked, peering down at Drawe curiously. The boy, still clutching at Deryna's skirts, refused to meet his eyes, but at least he hadn't run off. "He is Cousin Sharla's son? I didn't realize they'd had a child."

"Yes. I took him in when he was a wee babe." Deryna stroked his mop of dark red hair. "Come, Drawe. Say hello to your Uncle Iannis."

Drawe finally lifted his head. He stared as Iannis crouched down to meet him at eye level. "You're a very handsome young man," he said gently. "I can see your mother in you. She was a lovely woman."

Drawe lowered his gaze again. "Thank you," he mumbled. "I didn't know her, though."

"I'm sure you've heard stories about her," Iannis said solemnly. "I have quite a few from when we were children that I'd love to share with you when you have the time. Would you like that?"

The boy nodded. Iannis straightened, then offered him a hand. Drawe hesitated for a moment before he took it, and my heart melted as I watched the two of them head into the dining room. Iannis would be a great father when the time came.

Ennartha was regarding me doubtfully, as though still wondering what her son could see in me, but I couldn't be bothered to resent her just now. I was just so happy Iannis had come for me before his bitch of a grandmother sent me off on yet another life-threatening challenge. With any luck, we'd be out of here before dessert, and I'd finally get to sleep in my own bed.

I'm never taking my life for granted again, I decided as we sat down for dinner. Yes, it could be tedious and stressful at times, but at least back home I wasn't powerless and insignificant.

Despite Deryna's attempts at peacemaking, tension crackled in the air as we ate the meal that had been set out—pork roast, asparagus, and mashed potatoes. Glancing at Drawe, who was sitting next to Iannis, I refrained from recounting my ordeal and simply enjoyed the food.

"This is very good," Iannis said to Deryna in an attempt to

lighten things up. "I'd forgotten how good your cook is. I'll have to come and visit more often."

The air crackled and Ta'sradala reappeared in our midst. My food nearly went down the wrong pipe, and from the sudden silence, I knew everyone else was equally uneasy.

"Who says you are leaving at all?" she demanded. Ennartha paled, Deryna put a hand over her eyes, and Drawe cowered back in his chair. "Your bride has not passed my test. She has cheated at all of the challenges."

"You keep saying that, and Magorah help me, I'll figure out a way to rip that icy black heart out of your chest," I growled. "As I've said before, you never laid down any ground rules, so there's no way that I was cheating. You're just making shit up as you go along."

"Is that true?" Iannis asked pointedly. "You told Sunaya she had to pass some test and did not tell her the rules?"

"I assumed she knew them," Ta'sradala said haughtily. "Clearly I gave her too much credit."

"Mother," Ennartha said, her tone cajoling. "It is unlikely an ignorant mortal would automatically know your rules. Nobody here can support your claim that Sunaya cheated."

"I agree," Iannis said. "How many challenges has she completed?"

"Three," Deryna said before Ta'sradala could answer. "And they were all dangerous enough."

"Surely Sunaya and Iannis have proven their tenacity if nothing else," Ennartha said. "Perhaps we should let them return home and marry. Foolish or not, it is obvious that they are not going to be dissuaded from their course no matter what you say or do, Mother."

"I agree," Deryna said. "Let them be happy."

Ta'sradala looked like she wanted to object, but before she could, a male Tua appeared by her shoulder in a flash of light. Drawe screamed and hid under the table, which I couldn't blame him for—the Tua was huge, twelve feet of pure, masculine power. His silvery-blond head scraped the top of the ceiling, and that was *with* him shrinking down his form. He narrowed golden eyes on Ta'sradala, who stood up so quickly I barely registered the motion.

"Brother," she said in a deeply respectful voice, bowing. I stared —I couldn't believe that Ta'sradala would be subservient to anyone, but here she was, bowing before someone else! Ennartha was on her feet and bowing as well, and if not for the fact that Iannis and Deryna remained rooted in their chairs, I might have done the same.

"That is my Great Uncle R'gaolar," Iannis said in a shocked voice. *"The head of my grandmother's clan in the Tua realm."*

"Really?" I craned my neck, looking up at him with interest. *"You've met him when you visited the Tua realm, I'm guessing?"*

"No, he came to Recca once before, when I was very small. But that was an age ago."

"Sister," R'gaolar said, his voice cold. "I come seeking my youngest."

"Broghan?" Ta'sradala answered, sounding confused. "I have not seen him."

Cold horror spilled through me as I stared at the irate-looking Tua. Broghan was his *son*? By Magorah, I was in *so* much trouble. Anxiously, I called for the shape-shifter in mindspeak again, but he didn't answer. What the hell had happened to him? Was I going to be held accountable for his disappearance?

"He was visiting with two of his cousins when he vanished," R'gaolar said. "Right around the same time that this frail mortal of yours"—he flicked a hand at me—"came to visit. Perhaps *you* know where he is?" he asked, looking pointedly at me.

"I am sorry that he is missing," Ta'sradala said, and I could have sworn I heard a hint of fear in her voice. "But I truly have nothing to do with this."

"Forgive me if I find that hard to believe," R'gaolar said. "It is too much of a coincidence that you sent a mortal into our realm, *unsanctioned,* and then my son vanishes right after. I have spoken with Nalan and Alara, and they confirmed that she visited them. The Creator only knows how this outsider may have corrupted their young minds with her strange notions and vices."

I wanted to protest that insult but decided to keep my mouth shut—the last thing I needed was to get myself into more trouble. I hoped that Nalan and Alara weren't getting any flak for helping me out—did R'gaolar even know how much knowledge they'd given me? I assumed neither he nor Ta'sradala would be happy if they knew I now had the power to travel between the two realms. Not that I would risk it again without Broghan to help out.

"Is this how you repay our hospitality," R'gaolar hissed, turning the might of his piercing regard fully toward me now. "By stealing my son?"

My stomach clenched with fear, and I forced myself to relax. "I didn't steal him," I said, as calmly as I could. "It's not like I could control a Tua. He hitched a ride with me when I came back to Recca, and I didn't realize it until after we arrived. He said he wanted to see our world for himself, and he was with me on my last...adventure," I said, infusing that last word with sarcasm. "But he didn't come back with me when Ta'sradala yanked me back here, so I don't know where he went."

"I see," R'gaolar said softly. The look in his eyes told me that there would be hell to pay if Broghan was harmed in any way, and I started to sweat a little. The Tua made a complicated gesture and spoke what I recognized to be some kind of searching spell, thanks to my recent mastery of the Tua language. There was a loud POP, and Broghan came tumbling out of my sleeve in baby dragon form, landing in a heap on my half-eaten plate of food. The little scamp had been here all along? Hiding from Ta'sradala, I presumed, who had to be his aunt.

"I should have known," R'gaolar said dryly, no longer looking quite so angry now that his son was recovered. He switched to Tua. "Clean yourself up and stop playing about."

Broghan chuffed, then flew to the ground. There was a flash of light, and I blinked as he morphed into a young boy, similar in coloring to his father, though he only stood about eight feet tall. "I am not ready to return home yet," he said, a bit petulantly. "You never let me have fun."

"You are far too young for this particular kind of fun," R'gaolar said firmly. "What were you thinking, coming to this realm without so much as leaving a note? Everyone is out searching for you."

"I wanted an adventure," Broghan said defiantly, "and I got one. Besides, I was worried that Sunaya might not make it back in one piece, so I came along to make sure she arrived safely in her world. It's a good thing too, because she nearly died, and neither of you would have wanted that on your conscience, would you?" He met Ta'sradala's gaze, and she scowled and averted her eyes. Of course that was just what she had hoped for, but she knew better than to say it out loud, especially right now.

"While I'm sure the mortal appreciates your heroics, it was not your place to play knight in shining armor," R'gaolar growled. "You should not have run away. You know the punishment for disobedience." Huh. I wondered what kind of punishments Tua meted out to rebellious kids.

"I am still glad I came here," Broghan countered easily, not at all intimidated by his stern parent, "and I shall come back whenever I please, no matter how much of a fuss you all make. This realm is far too fascinating to leave unexplored!"

R'gaolar made an exasperated sound in the back of his throat, then grabbed Broghan by the arm. The two of them disappeared in another flash of light, leaving the rest of us staring at the spot where they'd vanished. The silence stretched on for several seconds as we tried to collect ourselves from the shock. Even Ta'sradala seemed shaken, with good reason—she'd just dodged a major bullet, thanks to me.

"Now that you've seen what comes of engaging in such reckless acts," Iannis said, finally breaking the silence, "it is really time that you let us go home, Grandmother. The wedding is mere days away, and we have much to prepare for."

"That is not my problem," Ta'sradala said stiffly. "You have offended this family by not consulting us before tying yourself to this mortal, and there must be consequences."

"If there *are* to be consequences," Iannis said heatedly, "then you should punish *me*, not Sunaya. She is entirely blameless in this situation."

"Iannis!" I protested, but he didn't look at me.

"You've already put me through hell and back," I snapped at Ta'sradala. "Don't you think you've done enough?"

"Please," Deryna said. "Let this go, Ta'sradala."

"Sunaya has proved her loyalty and devotion to Iannis," Ennartha said. "I give my blessing to her, and you should too, Mother."

Ta'sradala stared at us for a long moment, her face a stony mask. I could scent the strength of her hostility and convulsively gripped Iannis's hand under the table. Should I ask him to use the gulaya now, before she could open her mouth? But I didn't know if he would be fast enough—I certainly hadn't been, and now mine was sitting in my magical sleeve, dead and useless.

"I cannot deny that you have somehow made it through my challenges," Ta'sradala finally said, a crafty gleam in her eyes that made my stomach clench with apprehension. "But the true test of a marriage comes when a couple is forced to face adversity as one. I shall set you one more challenge that you two must complete together. If you survive *that*, you shall have my blessing."

"Why you—" I snarled, but the old Tua waved her hand before I could finish my sentence. The world began to spin again, and I grabbed Iannis tightly, terrified that we would be separated. Where was that old bitch sending us now? And would we be able to survive this final test?

17

"Great," I muttered when the world had finally stopped spinning. "This is just fucking great."

"I see my grandmother was particularly inspired with this locale," Iannis said dryly as we looked around. We stood in the middle of a vast desert, with absolutely nothing but red sand dunes and valleys as far as the eye could see. The sun blazed overhead in a yellowish sky, and the clouds were some kind of noxious green color. There were no signs of life, not so much as a single cactus jutting up from the sea of red death.

"Yeah, well I guess she thought I had it too easy with the underground caverns," I said. "At least that place had water, even if it was cold."

"Underground caverns?" Iannis raised an eyebrow. "That almost sounds exciting."

"It was for the first half hour or so. But after falling into a fissure and almost dying, the novelty wore off pretty quick."

Iannis smiled. "I missed you," he said, burying his face in my hair. My heart warmed as he held me tight against him, and I took a moment to enjoy his embrace as the hot winds gusted around us. We would have plenty of time to grumble and tear our hair out as we tried to escape this hellhole—I could take a few minutes to enjoy being reunited with Iannis again.

We sat down in the scant shade of a flat rock. "Tell me everything that happened," Iannis prompted. "I was terrified for you. Until I found you again, alive and well, I kept imagining terrible things— a thousand ways you could have perished, and I would have never known the truth about what happened." He squeezed my hand tightly. "I don't *ever* want to go through such an experience again."

"Me neither," I said fervently, squeezing his hand back. "Your grandmother decided that I was too weak to marry you, and she told me I had to pass three tests to prove I was worthy of you."

"How ridiculous." Iannis's eyes blazed with anger. "Whether or not you are 'worthy' is not up to her at all, and as far as I'm concerned we have both proved ourselves to each other a hundred times over."

I smiled. "Yeah, well you can tell that to the old bitch the next time you see her." I took a breath. "For the first test, she threw me into the cold, stormy sea, with only a rowboat to keep me afloat. I nearly drowned out there, but I managed to make it to a fishing vessel and get myself out of harm's way." I shivered, remembering how fucking cold I was. "I wonder how she knew when to yank me back. Is there some way for her to observe what I was doing? She clearly didn't see what I was doing in the Tua realm during my second challenge, and who I met there."

"I believe she can observe what happens as long as her victims are in Recca—but perhaps not if they are in other dimensions," Iannis speculated. "Or perhaps the Tua realm is shielded from eavesdropping, unlike other realms."

"Huh." I frowned. "If she can't eavesdrop in other dimensions, that means my third challenge was probably still in Recca."

"I can't believe my grandmother really sent you to the Tua realm." Iannis scowled. "But it is obvious she did—I guessed as much from that scene with the young Tua, though I could not understand what he and his father said to each other."

"I can understand them now," I said. "The trip was surprisingly...educational." I gave a lopsided smile at Iannis's astonished look.

He shook his head. "It's a miracle you survived the experience, if my memories of the place are at all accurate." He pulled me into his arms, and I sighed a little as I pressed my cheek against his broad chest. The steady thrum of his heartbeat soothed me, making me want to sink into his embrace and forget about our problems. From the comfort of his arms, I told him all about my adventures with the Tua, and my last ordeal in the underground caves.

"You were incredibly lucky that the Tua you ran across were benevolent," Iannis said gravely when I'd finished. "There are others who would have caged you up as a pet, or worse, roasted you over a spit and eaten you. And the forests contain other horrors you never saw—giant poisonous ants, flesh-eating birds, and a kind of vampire poltergeist, to name only a few I heard of from my mother."

I shuddered at the thought. "Yeah, I did get lucky. But aside from that one monster, and the quicksand, it wasn't that bad. And at least I can file that trip away as something I've done that no other living 'mortal' has experienced."

Iannis laughed. "I'm glad you are able to still see the bright side," he said, kissing the top of my head. "Though I wish I had been there, with you, rather than that erratic young shape-shifter."

"I'm sort of glad you didn't have to endure all that with me," I confessed, pressing my forehead against his. "Though I am happy to have you with me now."

I kissed him softly then, and Iannis tightened his arms around me, pulling me even closer as we finally took a moment to savor our alone time. No, it wasn't the most ideal location for a reunion, but after being separated from Iannis for so long I'd take what I could get. The taste of him as he slid his tongue into my mouth, the feel of his strong hands as they roamed up and down my back, his addictive sandalwood and magic scent... these were all things I'd begun to take for granted. I clung to him as we kissed languorously, taking our time to reaffirm our love for each other.

"I don't have anything nearly so exciting to report," Iannis said at last, when I pulled back to catch my breath. "The wedding preparations were still on schedule when I departed. Director

Chen promised to ensure that if we manage to get back in time, things should go off without a hitch."

With everything I'd experienced at Ta'sradala's hands so far, I wasn't quite so optimistic about our timely return. But I didn't see any reason to dash Iannis's hopes, so I stayed silent.

Iannis and I ate some jerky and took a swig out of my canteen, then took stock of our supplies. Thankfully, we had some usable items, like the blanket I'd brought, and a pair of sleeping bags that Iannis had stored away for emergencies, but there wasn't anything that could get us out of here, and our food and water stores wouldn't last us more than a few days.

"Where do you think we are?" I asked as the sun began to set. "The colors in this place seem strange, though not nearly as strange as the Tua realm."

"In yet another dimension, more than likely," Iannis said with a sigh. "For all we know this entire world is like this, with no food or water."

We used the levitation spell to float up high in the air, but even from hundreds of feet up, we couldn't see anything but desert. As the night sky came out, dotted with unfamiliar constellations, the light of the sun was replaced by the reflections of two huge yellow moons.

"Well that was useless," I said as we slowly drifted back to the ground. "I'm guessing your gulaya isn't going to work here, since we're not in Recca."

"I doubt it," Iannis agreed. "And I dare not risk trying, since I have no way to recharge it here. We will need to find some other method of escape."

We discussed various options on how to make this place more hospitable while we tried to figure out our escape, but even pooling our knowledge together, we came up empty. The spells to produce water relied on gathering moisture from the air, and there was none here. And while transmogrification was an option, it took quite a bit of magical energy and would have to be a last resort. Not to mention that with no food, we had to be careful not to expend our power any more than was absolutely necessary.

Exhausted from his travels, Iannis curled up next to me on his sleeping bag and fell asleep. I tried to catch some z's too, but my mind was buzzing, too wired to settle down. As I stared up at the strange night sky, I sorted through the knowledge the Tua had given me. Would I be able to walk from this dimension back to Recca? I had done it before, but that was because Nalan and Alara had known the precise path, and I had been able to follow it. Plus, I'd only survived thanks to Broghan's help. This time, I had no idea which dimension I was in, and in what direction Recca lay. If I tried to travel at random, I might accidentally transport us to another realm even more inhospitable than this. We could land in a world with toxic air, unable to breathe, or beneath an ocean, and die from the water pressure. Not to mention that the spell used up so much energy —I'd be totally depleted and weak as a kitten, vulnerable to any passing predator, unable to try again if I got it wrong the first time.

Except this time, you have Iannis with you. Between the two of you, you might be able to pull it off.

The hope that we might actually have a viable way of getting home—even if the plan wasn't fully formed—was enough to help my mind finally relax. I slept for a few hours curled up next to Iannis, stirring sometime later when sunlight began to creep beneath my eyelids.

"Iannis," I mumbled when I felt him shift next to me. "I have an idea about how to get us out of here."

"You do?" Iannis asked, sounding fully awake. I opened my eyes to see him staring at me, looking intrigued. "How?"

"Nalan and Alara gave me the knowledge on how to walk between dimensions," I explained. "That was how I was able to make it back to Recca. I only have the exact instructions on how to get from the Tua realm to our world, but I assume the process could be used to walk between any two dimensions, if only we can figure out the way. However, it takes a huge amount of power, and I was completely drained the last time. And since I'm not sure where we are, I'm worried that we might accidentally end up in a different world instead of back home. If it's not one that we can find food and water on, we'll die before we can try again."

"It will be dangerous," Iannis agreed, his brow furrowed. "But we don't have any alternative, do we? At least with our combined power we should be able to travel without draining you."

"I hope so. Once we leave here, Ta'sradala may not be able to find us again," I said. "She's probably watching us gleefully as we struggle. Do you think she'd bring us back before we die of thirst or hunger? I know she hates me, but she might save you, at least."

"I wouldn't count on it," Iannis said. "And if she brought me back after I'd watched you perish, I'd rather not return at all. Anything, any risk, is better than that."

I bit my lip. "Do you think we should try it now?" I asked, sitting up.

Iannis shrugged. "Why wait? The longer we stay here, the more we will suffer in this heat anyway. Now, while we are still strong and well-fed, we have the best chance of success."

We quickly packed up our sleeping bags and canteens in our magical sleeves, then joined hands. Anxiety welled up inside me, and I leaned in to kiss Iannis again.

"If we don't come out in one piece on the other end," I murmured against his lips, "please know that I love you, and that I have no regrets."

"I do know," he said, nuzzling my cheek. "As certainly as I know that the sun rises and sets. Or at least it does in our world. And I love you just as much, if not more. Now let's begin."

Iannis put a protective bubble around us, enclosing a supply of the hot but breathable air in case we got stuck in the void, or someplace else that was inhospitable. Once I was certain the bubble was secure, I reached for the knowledge the Tua had given me and pulled out the dimension-walking spell. As I studied the directions again, Iannis began to pour some of his power into me, filling me up with sizzling hot magic. I took a deep breath as it flowed in my veins and let the map of the dimensions fall open into my mind again. I could see where Recca was, and the Tua realm, but I had no idea which square of the quilt we were on, and another tremor of fear went through me. What if I fucked this up?

"Relax," Iannis said to me in mindspeak. *"Let your instincts guide you."*

Nodding, I zeroed in on the square that was Recca, and spoke the spell, willing it to take us back home. The world shifted and tilted around me, and I clutched Iannis's hands tightly as I felt my magic pour out of me once again. Opening my eyes, I saw a swirl of colors, and my heart leapt. Was it working this time? Would we actually make it back?

Our feet slammed into the ground, and I stumbled into Iannis. He caught me before I fell, and I sucked in a deep breath of the hot air in our bubble. My heart sank—we were in the middle of a prairie. But not just any prairie. The tall grass, which nearly came up to my knees, was a deep indigo color, and the sky above us was bright orange. Off in the distance a herd of what looked like bison was grazing, but they seemed to be a dark green, the color of evergreen trees, and something was off about their shape.

"I'm afraid this isn't Recca," Iannis said, voicing the obvious. "But at least there is life in this world. Better than what we had before."

"There is that," I said, letting out a gusty sigh. "Let me test the air, see if it's breathable."

Iannis protested, but I had already taken a few steps forward, leaving the bubble. Cool air wafted against my skin, and I took in a deep breath, then let it out in a sigh of relief when nothing bad happened. The air seemed to be just fine here, and with a tang of grass and moisture, it was ten times better than that hot desert air we'd been breathing before.

I signaled to Iannis to drop the air bubble, then raked a hand through my hair, trying to ground myself. I felt woozy from using all that magic, and I pulled another piece of beef jerky from my sleeve and munched on it as I looked around.

"I guess we can hunt those things, whatever they are," I said, pointing at the herd off in the distance.

"I'd rather find something smaller," Iannis said as he came to stand by my side. "There are probably rabbits and deer, or something like them anyway."

I bit my lip, fighting back the surge of disappointment that threatened to overwhelm me. "I guess we need to replenish our energy before we try the spell again," I said forlornly.

Iannis put an arm around my shoulder and kissed the top of my head. "Don't despair," he murmured against my scalp. "We'll figure this out. And just look how far you've come as a mage. Did you ever think you would end up traveling to different worlds?"

"No," I admitted, leaning into his embrace. "If we ever get out of this, we'll have some great stories to tell our children."

Iannis hugged me a little tighter at that. "Yes, we will. And our grandchildren too, though I doubt they'll believe us when they get older. Now let's find something to eat, and some shelter."

I shifted quickly into panther form, then took off through the grass at a trot, intent on exploring while Iannis set off to find a place to camp. At this level, it was easy to pick up the various scent trails, and in no time, I caught a scent very similar to rabbit, though there was an appetizing clover-like odor mixed in it. My mood picked up as I followed it for a good half mile, then soured as I found its burrow. I didn't need to dig into it to scent the litter huddled beneath it, or the tiny animals' fear. No matter how hungry I was, I wasn't going to kill a mother and leave her babies to starve.

The next scent trail I picked up was more promising—a small group of deer, just two miles south of the weird bison herd I'd seen earlier. The bison themselves were tempting, but I didn't think I could take them down without the help of magic, and the deer were much easier. I killed a young, yellow-furred male with very little effort, then used a levitation spell to bring it back to Iannis.

Thankfully, our serapha charms were working once again, and I was able to find Iannis quickly. He'd made camp at the top of a hill, not too far from the forest, and already had a good fire going.

"That was fast," Iannis said as I changed back into human form. "You were gone for little over an hour."

"I was motivated," I said with a smile as I set to helping him skin and gut the animal for dinner. "After being separated against our will, I have no intention of letting you out of my sight any longer than necessary."

"The feeling is entirely mutual," he said with a tender smile that made my stomach flip-flop.

We roasted the deer over the fire, then used the pile of large branches and leaves Iannis had gathered to build a shelter for the evening. The meat was juicier than I expected—the deer in this world were fattier than the ones on Recca. Soon enough, we were lying back on our sleeping bags in the tent, listening to the fire crackle as we snuggled.

"If we try not to think about it too much, we can almost pretend that we're on our honeymoon," Iannis said, and I laughed.

"I'd envisioned white beaches rather than camping in the woods, but this will do in a pinch," I said, skimming my hand through his long hair. It felt so good to have him back, and as he stroked a hand gently down my side, my skin began to heat. "I don't see any reason why we can't celebrate," I purred, moving closer.

Iannis slipped his arm around me, and our mouths met in a deep, passionate kiss. We took it slow, with soft, loving kisses, and I let myself melt into him, forgetting about the worries of the world. His strong muscles flexed beneath my hands as I rubbed slow circles around his back, and then he rolled me over, trailing more kisses along the edge of my jaw, then down my neck.

"It feels like an age since I've last made love to you," he

murmured against my collarbone. I felt a tingle of magic, and then suddenly our clothes were gone and we were skin to skin. I arched my hips into his hard length, and he pressed me back down with a growl, biting down. I moaned as his hand slid between my legs, where I was already wet and aching, and I opened readily for him.

"Yes," I moaned as his thumb found my sweet spot. He slid two fingers inside me as he stroked my clit, and I came almost immediately, arching off the ground again as pleasure speared through me. I scored my nails down his back as he kept going, using those talented fingers to drive me wild as he sucked one of my nipples into his mouth. I was on fire, a deep hunger clawing me from the inside, and I wanted to wrap myself up in him until I didn't know where he began and I ended.

"Please," I panted after he'd sent me over the edge again. I reached for his cock, and he hissed as I gently began to stroke him. "I want you inside me."

"More," he said, wrapping his hand around mine and urging me faster. I kissed him hard as he did, loving the feel of him in my hand as I tasted him. He groaned into my mouth, and I took advantage of the distraction, rising up to flip him onto his back.

"Gotcha," I said with a grin as I slowly lowered myself onto him. We both moaned as he filled me completely, stretching me until I was both satisfied and aching for more. Bracing my hands on his rock-solid chest, I began to rock up and down, gently at first, then faster as the pleasure began to build inside me. Iannis's eyes blazed, his violet irises taking on a warm glow from the flickering fire, and he gripped my hips, pushing me faster as he thrust.

I leaned down for a kiss, and he grabbed my ass and ground my hips against his hardness, triggering another climax. I groaned into his mouth as I shook with pleasure, holding on for dear life as he continued to pound into me. Warmth filled me as he came inside me with a rush, and his body stiffened beneath mine in joyful release.

Sighing, I collapsed against him, and we lay there in silence, panting as we worked to catch our breath. His heart hammered against my ear as I traced patterns through the light dusting of hair on his chest, and as his heartbeat evened out, it became a comforting sound lulling me to sleep.

"I love you," Iannis said softly as he stroked my hair. I mumbled that I loved him too, then fell asleep to the sound of the fire crackling and his slow, steady breathing. There would be time enough to worry about our circumstances tomorrow—for now, just being here with him was enough.

18

The next morning, I awoke to the sensation of something warm and heavy sliding along my leg. At first, I thought it was simply Iannis rubbing his foot against my calf, but the *something* began to wrap around my leg in a way that a human leg *definitely* wasn't capable of.

"What the..." I mumbled blearily as I pulled the blanket aside. My eyes widened as a bright yellow snake lifted his massive triangular head and flicked his forked tongue at me. "Fuck!" I yelled, trying to leap to my feet, but the snake squeezed harder, preventing me from getting up.

"What is it?" Iannis shouted, jolting upright. He swore at the sight of the boa, who was rapidly winding itself around my body, though luckily my arms were still free. The giant reptile was halfway up my torso when my brain finally kicked in, and I pulled one of my crescent knives, then grabbed the snake by the throat and impaled him with the long end of the weapon.

"Eww," I groaned as black blood splashed all over my face. I gagged as I accidentally got some in my mouth, and turned my head to spit it out.

"Well, that was quite a scare," Iannis said as he pulled the now limp snake off my body. The reptile was very heavy, a good twelve feet long and six inches around, and I shuddered in disgust as I watched Iannis drag the carcass out of the tent. "Do you think we should have it for breakfast?" he called over his shoulder.

"Ha. Ha." I rolled my eyes, then got to my feet and took stock of myself. Thankfully I hadn't been wearing my clothes, but the snake blood had gotten all over our sleeping bags. I used a cleaning spell to take care of the stains, then pulled on my clothes as Iannis came back into the tent.

"Is that really necessary?" he asked, still buck-naked himself. "It isn't as if there's anyone around to see us."

I laughed. "We can't spend all day having sex," I said. "And besides, I'd rather not be naked when the next predator comes by to eat me."

"True," Iannis agreed as he donned his robe. "It seems the fire wasn't enough to warn them off. I'll have to put a protection spell around the perimeter."

We cut off some of the leftover deer and broke our fast as we watched the quasi-bison graze in the distance—Iannis and I decided to call them "quasis" for short.

"How were you able to get away from Solantha at a time like this?" I asked. "I know you've got Chen to run things in your absence, but with the Convention about to start, and you gone, she must be pulling her hair out."

"Yes, and I feel bad about leaving her alone to deal with that mess," Iannis said. "But without you, there can be no wedding, and the Convention is of little import to me. Of course I had to come after you."

"How did you know that I was in Manuc?" I asked. "Were you able to sense me? The serapha charms weren't working before. Ta'sradala must have done something to them."

Iannis shook his head. "They didn't work for me either, and I was terrified that meant you were dead. Luckily, Liu saw you being pulled into the pool—she was hiding in a cherry tree nearby. From the way she described the scene, I gathered someone with incredible power had to have taken you, and the list of suspects was short enough. No living mage could have done it."

"Not even you?"

"Not even me. Coupled with the recent letter from my mother, Manuc seemed like the most likely place to start looking. In fact, Aunt Deryna sent a message warning me of what had happened that found me just as I was embarking on the east coast." He looked grave. "She warned me to prepare for the worst—that it was unlikely I'd still find you alive. It is a good thing she underestimated you, as so many have done before."

I grimaced. "No, her prognosis was pretty spot-on. I'm very lucky to be alive. Your grandmother definitely didn't intend for me to survive those awful tests. And now that she sent you off to that horrible desert with me, I can't imagine she cares for anyone at all. All that bluster about you being part of the family...I have to wonder how she treats her enemies, if this is how she acts toward her loved ones." I shook my head in disgust.

Iannis laughed sharply. "At least now you know why I don't like to speak of my Tua heritage. I've often wished my mother were an ordinary mage or even human. My greatest ambition is to be as unlike Ta'sradala and her ilk as possible."

"When you consider how helpless we were against Tua power, maybe you can better understand the resentment of ordinary humans and shifters against mages."

Iannis frowned. "It is not at all the same. We are not congenitally capricious and amoral—"

I raised an eyebrow. "In some cases, it is *exactly* alike, especially from the victims' point of view."

Iannis was silent for a while, but the frown lingered.

"Besides, not all Tua are evil like Ta'sradala, no matter how powerful they are compared to us," I continued on, mollifying my accusation a bit. "The younger ones I met were a lot more reasonable and actually helped me survive. I think you were just unlucky to get stuck with Ta'sradala as your ancestor."

"Very likely," Iannis admitted. "Kidnapping my grandfather was rather outrageous, even for her race."

"In any case, I'm very glad you found me, even if we are stuck in this place," I said, squeezing his hand. "Now we just have to figure out how to get out of here."

He brightened at that. "Once we can get back to Recca, we can use my gulaya to go straight home," Iannis said. "But we need to figure out how to ensure the dimension spell takes us there rather than somewhere else. We got lucky last time, landing in a world with breathable air and food, but we may not the next time around."

"I wish I could transmit the dimension walking spell, the way the Tua did to me," I said. "There are...technical aspects that I don't understand, and I'm not sure I even have the words to put them into human language. I feel like if we could just figure out the formula behind the magic, we could direct the spell to where we want it to go."

Iannis frowned. "The only way I know of doing that is the knowledge transfer."

I bit my lip at that. I wasn't sure I wanted to do a knowledge transfer—I knew how the spell worked, thanks to Fenris's knowledge, and it could only be done once. If the transfer was successful, Iannis would have access to my entire lifetime of memories. Fenris was incredibly brave and selfless to give me access to his past—if I scoured them thoroughly enough, I could access his most intimate secrets, his most humiliating moments, recollections of all the stupid things he had said and done over the long decades of his life. I did not want to know all that about Iannis, and would have refused if he'd offered. Was I really willing to give Iannis that same power over me? I trusted him with my life, but could our upcoming marriage survive if I exposed myself so completely to him? I would have to live with him afterward, knowing that he had intimate knowledge of everything about me, that I had no secrets left.

"I'm not sure that I'm ready to do that," I said cautiously. "Not unless there really is no other option."

Iannis nodded. "I don't blame you. It is a big step, and irrevocable."

We spent another two days and nights out on that prairie as we tried to figure out the solution. This time we hunted down one of the quasis, knowing the meat would last us much longer than a deer. The herd of giant bovines were unafraid when we approached in human form, telling us that they had never been hunted by our kind, but the moment I changed into a panther and sprang for the weakest among them, an older quasi with a marked limp, they scattered. Between my hunting prowess and Iannis's magic, we were able to bring down the lame quasi easily enough, and we enjoyed its meat even as the novelty of our surroundings began to wear off.

On the third morning, as I sipped a weak tea we'd brewed from some prairie flowers that Iannis had determined were safe to ingest, I sorted through the knowledge the Tua had given me for what seemed like the millionth time. On a whim, I gathered it all together, then repacked it into the shining trunk it had come in, conjuring it again in my mind's eye from wherever it had disappeared to.

I wonder if I can replicate the trunk in my mind, I thought as I drummed my fingers against my thigh. I held the knowledge in my mind's eye and concentrated, willing a duplication to form. To my delight, the trunk blurred, then split apart into two separate ones.

"Iannis," I called. "Come here a second!"

"What is it?" he asked, moving away from the fire he'd been tending. He crouched down beside me, his brow furrowed in curiosity. "Have you found something?"

"I think so," I said, pressing two fingers against that furrowed brow. I felt the knowledge pass between my mind and into Iannis's, and he gasped, his violet eyes going wide.

"Did it work?" I asked, breathless with excitement. "Can you see the spell now?"

"I believe I can," Iannis said wonderingly. He sat down with a *thump* in the grass next to me and stared off into the distance, unseeing. "Yes, I can see what you meant about the technical aspects of this spell. This is going to take some time for me to puzzle out."

"But you *can* puzzle it out, right?" I asked eagerly. Was this it? Were we finally going to be able to get home?

"Yes," he said impatiently as he pulled out a leather-bound book and a pen from his magical sleeve. His eyes gleamed, alight with the joy of a difficult challenge as he opened the book and began to scribble. "No wonder you had trouble with the technical part

..." he murmured after a minute. "It would seem the Tua use an entirely different system of mathematics than we do."

"Do you think you can crack it?" I asked eagerly.

"I certainly hope so." He didn't even look up at me. "Now give me some peace and quiet. I have work to do."

19

Iannis spent the rest of the day scribbling down formulas in his notebook, then scratching them out. I busied myself making things out of the parts of the quasi we had saved—Fenris's outdoorsman knowledge included instructions on how to magically tan hides and use the leather to make clothing and bedding, how to craft weapons and tools from the horns and bones, and even ways to use the hair and sinew to make thread, headdresses, and ornaments. Fenris had culled some of the spells from the antique memoirs of mage explorers and pioneers who had first traversed and settled the area of the Federation, and since he remembered everything he ever read, I spent some time revisiting those old accounts. By the time lunch came around, I'd successfully turned the quasi horns into a set of spear handles and had several large pieces of hard leather.

Not exactly useful, but it kept my mind off my impatience to go home, so I could give Iannis space to work.

"I think I am getting closer with each iteration," Iannis said as we wolfed down a quasi-bison stew I'd made using some herbs and tubers I'd found while foraging in the woods the previous day. "If I am able to figure this out, what we have been given is going to revolutionize both physics and mathematics. And as for the practical applications..." His eyes shone with the possibilities despite his frustration, and I had to smile.

"I'm sure you and Elnos will be holed up in your study for days, once we finally get home," I said. "The two of you are going to become mad scientists together."

"Inventors," Iannis corrected with a smile. "And we'll probably publish a number of papers that should interest all the universities on Recca. Unfortunately, figuring out how to apply this knowledge to travel between dimensions practically, and safely for that matter, is proving more difficult than I anticipated. I need to get it right—now that I know more, I understand just how risky our last jump was. We are very lucky to be alive."

After we'd finished eating, I kissed Iannis and let him return to his work while I cleaned up and continued my leather-working experiment. I felt downright domestic, taking care of all the cooking and cleaning and other "housework" while he slaved away with that formula. While I'd done pretty well at math in school, I'd never studied the more advanced techniques necessary to understand those Tua equations.

Besides, there was something satisfying about working with my hands. I could never be a housewife or artisan, I decided, not for the rest of my life. But I didn't mind it just this second.

I was just finishing off a belt I'd made from one of the strips of leather when Iannis suddenly cried, "I have it!"

Dropping my craft project, I twisted around to see him holding up the book triumphantly, the latest formula scribbled across it. His eyes shone, and he was grinning broadly.

"Yes!" I jumped up from where I was sitting and raced over to him so I could give him a hug. "I knew you could do it! Do you want to try it right now?"

"Let's eat first and pack up whatever we want to take with us," Iannis suggested. "We are going to need all our strength, and if this goes wrong again, I want to be better prepared."

We packed up our supplies, then quickly ate some of the dried quasi. "I'll need to borrow your energy this time," Iannis said, taking my hands. "You've gotten significantly stronger since you disappeared," he added with a smile. "We are very nearly equal now, stronger than most mages I have ever met. A lot of them would be frightened of you, if they had any idea."

"That's thanks to the Tua power boost," I said as I curled my fingers around him. "I really ought to thank Nalan and Alara if I ever see them again. I wouldn't have survived without them, or Broghan either."

Iannis pressed a quick kiss against my lips, then spoke the spell he'd worked out. I sucked in a breath as I felt a strong tug at my power, and our hands lit up as my magic began flowing into him. Suddenly, we were yanked forward, the prairie around us disappearing into a swirling kaleidoscope of colors. Iannis and I clung to each other tightly as we hurtled through time and space, and I buried my face in his chest as I began to feel dizzy. Unlike last time, which seemed to only take a few seconds, the experience seemed to stretch out endlessly, until I began to panic, wondering if we'd somehow gotten stuck again and would never come back out.

"Relax," Iannis said in mindspeak. *"We are on the right track. The two dimensions are not closely aligned, which is why it takes longer."*

I blew out a long breath, forcing myself to let go, to trust that Iannis knew what he was doing. He'd never led me astray before. He would get us through this, just like he did with everything else.

Finally, we began to slow down, the pressure squeezing in on all sides gradually alleviating. Lifting my head, I saw that the colors swirling around us were beginning to meld, and as I stared, the landscape around us solidified into an endless landscape of yellow grasses and scattered trees. The air was hot, the sun beating down mercilessly on us, but it looked normal, and the sky surrounding it was a clear blue.

"A savannah," Iannis said, still holding me tight. "And those are gazelles off in the distance. I do believe we are in Faricia."

"Yes!" I pumped a fist in the air, and that was when a tribe of dark-skinned natives charged out from behind a clump of nearby trees. They wore skirts garnished with some kind of white and black fur, and their bodies were painted with clay in elaborate patterns. I drew my crescent knives as they pointed long spears at us, and Iannis threw up a shield. The natives hissed as the air around us shimmered with magic, and they jabbed at the shield angrily. They didn't seem happy to see us here, and what was worse, Iannis's shield wobbled beneath their blows. I tried to fortify it with my own magic, but after that transportation spell, we were almost tapped out. A wave of nausea swept through me, and it took everything I had to keep upright as my stomach twisted into knots.

"Damn," Iannis murmured as another native came forward from behind the trees. This one was taller than the others, with an elaborate headdress and several colorful amulets dangling from his neck and furs. He pressed his weathered hands against the shield and spoke in a strong, resonant voice. The shield flickered, then died, leaving us completely exposed.

"Please," I said, the word coming out in a strange language that I couldn't recall ever speaking. *"Don't hurt us. We mean you no harm."*

The man's eyes widened. *"You speak our language?"*

"Yes," I said, without missing a beat. I realized that Nalan and Alara had gifted me with the ability to understand and speak any language, not just Tua. *"We are travelers blown off course, just trying to return to our home."*

"Do not hurt them," the man, who I guessed was their shaman, said to the others. *"I wish to find out more about these pale-skinned travelers who have appeared so suddenly in our midst. They are weak just now, and easily within my power to control."*

"This isn't good," Iannis said to me in mindspeak as the shaman began to engage in a spirited debate with another native, who looked to be the hunt leader, about what to do with us. The hunt

leader pointed out, reasonably enough, that one killed enemies when they were weak, and that it might not be prudent to keep strange mages around any longer than necessary. Apparently, there were very strict rules about that in their tribal customs. *"They are just as likely to treat us as honored guests as they are to sacrifice us to whatever god they believe in."*

From what I'd overheard, the latter was a far more likely outcome. *"Great,"* I said, surreptitiously sidling closer to Iannis. *"Maybe now would be a good time to get the hell out of here?"*

Iannis quickly grabbed my arm, then pulled out the gulaya from his sleeve and activated it. The natives turned to us, shouting, and the last thing I saw was the astonished looks on their faces as we disappeared in a flash of light.

20

The moment our feet landed on solid ground, I dropped to my hands and knees and threw up in the nearest clump of bushes. They happened to be rose bushes, and familiar ones at that—even through my retching, I could tell that we were back in the gardens of Solantha Palace.

"Are you all right?" Iannis asked as he gently rubbed my back. *How come* he *doesn't get nauseous after gulaya travel?* I wondered, more than a little envious at his composure.

"I'll be fine," I gasped, wiping my mouth with the back of my hand. I pulled out my canteen from my sleeve and took a swig of cool water—*water from another dimension*, I thought wonderingly—to drown out the acrid taste. "All that traveling was just a little too much on my system," I said as I straightened.

"I know what you mean," Iannis said. Even he looked a bit unwell, his face paler than usual. But his eyes were bright with excitement as he looked around. "We've made it back, though, haven't we? There were some moments I doubted we would."

"We definitely have." Grinning, I flung my arms around him and squeezed tight. "Even better, we're finally free of Ta'sradala! She did say she wouldn't come after us if we survived that last trap she set for us." Not that she'd expected us to ever get home. She probably thought we were wasting away in that desert right now. It gave me great pleasure to have finally gotten the best of her.

"Indeed." Iannis's eyes sparkled with satisfaction. "After being bested again and again, she won't want to continue this confrontation. With any luck, we won't meet her again for at least a century."

"Or *ever*," I said hopefully, though that was probably too optimistic.

A gardener chose that moment to walk around the corner. He dropped the shovel he was carrying, his eyes widening in astonishment. "Lord Iannis! Miss Baine! You're back!"

"And here comes the cavalry," Iannis murmured as the guards came running from their posts to greet us. We were quickly escorted inside the palace amidst loud cheers. I did my best not to cringe at all the eyes fixed on us as we entered the building—after all that solitude, the gawking crowd was a bit disorienting. Every mage we passed wanted to know where we'd been, if we were all right, why we looked all dirty and disheveled, but Iannis and I deflected their questions as we headed straight for his rooms. There would be time enough to give explanations and get reports on what had been going on at home—for now, I was so tired that all I longed for was soaking in a hot bath and taking a long nap. And not necessarily in that order.

We were almost at Iannis's suite when a familiar voice echoed in my mind. *"Iannis?"* Fenris asked, sounding tentative. *"Sunaya?"*

Iannis and I froze, giving each other startled looks. *"Fenris?"* I cried, my heart leaping. Could it really be he? Here, in our home?

A few seconds later, Fenris's door, which was just a few feet from where we were standing, burst open. I squealed as Fenris rushed out—he looked exactly the same as when I'd last seen him, though he wore modern clothes instead of his usual tunics. My exhaustion forgotten, I shot across the hall to wrap him up in a bear hug.

"Dammit, Fenris!" I yelled as he returned the hug just as fiercely. "I missed you so fucking much," I mumbled into his shirt. Tears stung at my eyes as I lifted my head to look up at him, and my throat swelled with emotion as his yellow eyes blazed with happiness. Taking in a breath, I savored his familiar scent...and caught another one that smelled of magic and lavender and sunshine. "Figures you would take advantage of the quake to ditch us and go find a mate," I said, flashing him a grin. "I can smell her all over you."

Fenris cleared his throat, looking a little embarrassed. "We're not actually married yet," he said, stepping back. "Though I hope to be, soon."

"You must invite us to the wedding," Iannis said, sweeping in for a quick, hard hug of his own. "I'm so glad you will be here for ours."

"I wouldn't miss it for the world," Fenris said with a broad smile. He looked us both over, then said, "You both look exhausted. I'll let you rest, and we can talk more in the morning."

"Oh, hell no," I said, grabbing his arm. "You just got back—I'm not letting you out of my sight so soon." After all this time away, he was just going to leave us? I had an irrational fear that if I allowed that, he'd vanish again, perhaps for good.

"Technically *you* are the ones who just got back," Fenris said as I dragged him into the suite. I noticed he wasn't putting up any resistance. "I've been here in Solantha for several days."

"You have?" I exclaimed as we sat down in front of the fireplace. The door opened almost immediately, and I sighed a little in relief when a group of servants came in and set drinks and snacks down on the coffee table. My stomach rumbled, and I quickly snatched up some smoked ham—I was famished. "What have you been doing here this whole time?"

"I came here to warn you," Fenris said, helping himself to a glass of wine and a small plate of cheese and crackers. "There was a plot afoot—some of Thorgana's former associates were gathering ex-Resistance members here in Solantha and planned to seize the city after attacking the Convention in force. They hoped to kill the country's strongest mages in one go and improve their chances of seizing power. Luckily, they were discovered just today, their leaders imprisoned and their weapons seized. It was an impressive collaboration of the Mages

Guild under Director Chen, the enforcers, and Director Toring's office."

Iannis and I exchanged alarmed glances. "It would seem we've missed quite a bit," he said.

"And you, too?" I asked Fenris. He made it sound like everyone else had been involved, but I knew him better than that. "There is a tinge of gunpowder in your scent."

"I was there," he admitted. "Now that I have been outed as Lord Polar's illegitimate son, Garrett Toring has been surprisingly pleasant," he added wryly.

I chuckled. "So you know about that, huh? I hope you're not too offended—I kind of came up with it on the spur of the moment, and since I thought you were dead at the time, I didn't think there would be any ramifications to you."

Fenris smiled. "It was inspired, but you'll need to tell me every detail of your invention, so I don't accidentally give myself away."

"Never mind all that now. I want to know more about this plot," Iannis said, his violet eyes narrowed. "I knew there was a chance something like this could happen when the Minister announced he'd hold the Convention here. We took precautions, but we hadn't gotten wind of anything like this before I left."

The door opened before Fenris could reply, and Director Chen strode in. "Thank Resinah you are back," she said fervently in a rare show of emotion, making a beeline for Iannis. "I was beginning to reach my wits' end. Are you both unharmed?"

"Yes, thank you." Iannis smiled. "I apologize for leaving you hanging, Director Chen, but I trust you've had things in hand. I gather that on top of everything else, you had to deal with this Resistance plot Fenris was telling us about?"

Director Chen nodded, taking a seat in one of the empty chairs. "Fenris sent an anonymous warning on his way here, but it was not taken seriously. We acted quickly, however, after he connected with Director Toring. Fenris helped me get the crucial information out of the main suspect, Moredo, another of those construction tycoons... was that only six hours ago? It seems longer." She passed a hand over her brow in a weary gesture. "Then he also helped take care of the plotters, just in time for your return."

"You all did very well," Iannis said. "I am glad everything is in hand."

"Who else was involved?" I asked, leaning forward. "Did you find out anything about the details of the planned attack?"

Fenris and Director Chen fully briefed us on the particulars. I tried to listen attentively, but as I sat on the comfy couch, curled up against Iannis's warm body, I began to feel sleepy again. It seemed like we'd missed all the excitement—thanks to Fenris and Mina's sleuthing, and Director Chen and Garrett's quick action, the perpetrators had been apprehended. Even better, everything was still on schedule despite our long absence, so there was truly nothing to worry about.

"I'm glad you are able to go around Solantha in your own face once again," I said to Fenris after Chen had left, called away by an urgent appointment. "Sorry we weren't here when you first arrived. Your run-in with Garrett must have been scary as hell since you didn't know what I'd told him."

"How exactly did you run into him?" Iannis asked. "What did you say?"

"He helped me out of a tight spot in jail," Fenris admitted. "I was snooping around downtown when an enforcer arrested me on the orders of some gang or criminal businessman he was working with. He falsely charged me with trying to cheat a brothel owner."

I snorted with laughter. "A brothel owner? Just what kind of snooping were you doing?" I teased.

"Not that kind," Fenris said dryly, not taking the bait. "Anyway, Director Toring found out that I was in jail, and he took pity on me and sprung me. Believe it or not, he actually took me out to dinner, then told me that my parents were in town and that I should visit them." He shook his head. "I still have to go and see them. I have to admit that I'm not entirely looking forward to that visit, since they believe me to be my own son."

"They came here first, and I was sorry I could not help them," Iannis said. "They will eventually find out that you have resurfaced. Better that you go and see them in person than having them find out from a third party."

"I'm so glad that Garrett bought the story," I said, relieved. "He seemed convinced when I spun it, but that was months ago and I wasn't sure how he'd react if he ever saw you again. I tried to make you sound like a poor victim of your parents' indiscretion, brought up by your old great-uncle in that remote country house of his, and hidden away behind the library sofas whenever he had a visitor. I told him you grew up in that library, which explained your love of books and scholarship, and why you were so different from other shifters."

"It's a bit insulting how readily he and my parents believed your story," Fenris said with a frown. "I would never have treated any child of mine like that, shifter or no. But never mind all that," he added with a smile. "I am very happy you did this. Now that I am engaged to Mina, it means that the two of us should be able to live openly together. And my interest in ancient magical lore and my knowledge of Loranian no longer need to be hidden. I can even practice magic to some extent."

"And wear robes, if you want to," Iannis said. "That old great-uncle could have apprenticed you."

"I wish that you'd brought your Mina with you," I lamented. "I *really* want to meet her. She smells nice, Fenris—like lavender and sunshine. I bet she's one of those sweet and gentle types."

Fenris grinned. "She is, but she does have a fiery side if provoked. She is very excited about meeting the both of you, although she is a bit nervous."

"She won't have any need to be," Iannis assured him. "We'll make her feel right at home. I don't know that we'll have much time for social affairs before our wedding, what with everything going on, but we'll have to get together before you two leave."

"*Leave*?" I demanded. "You're not going back to whatever cave you've been hiding in, are you, Fenris?"

"Not permanently," Fenris admitted, "but Mina and I do need to settle our affairs in Watawis—that's where I ended up. We are thinking of moving back out to Canalo, but it will likely be nearby, and not within Solantha itself. Mina is very fond of the beach. And speaking of traveling, where in Recca did you two disappear off to? I heard that you might have gone to Manuc, but nobody knew for sure. What was so important that you had to leave at a crucial time like this?"

"It's a long story," Iannis said as I grimaced. The last thing I wanted to do was recount those painful experiences, not when the memories were still so fresh. "I'll have to tell you the details when I have more time, but in short, we had trouble with some of my Tua relatives. They were not pleased with my choice of a bride and would not be ignored on the matter."

I snorted. "That's the understatement of the year," I said, rolling my eyes. "Thankfully we managed to escape, and just in time, too. There's still so much to be done." I sighed, flopping back down onto the couch. I was so tired...

"I should go and find Mina," Fenris said, noting the way I slumped against Iannis. "You two look like you need to rest."

"All right," I said sleepily. "You said you were staying at the Marwale, right?"

"Yes," he said.

"That's much too far away," Iannis protested. "You and your friends must come stay here in the palace tonight. It's getting late for such a long drive."

"I agree," I said before Fenris could argue. "I'll have a suite readied for you and will tell the staff to expect you. Tell Com I said hi, and that I'll come see him when I'm alive again."

———

ALONE AT LAST, I snuggled with Iannis on the couch. "Can we just sleep here?" I mumbled into his chest. "I don't wanna move."

"We'll be waking up with aching backs if we do," he said, scooping me into his arms. "I see no need for that when we have a big bed waiting for us."

I wrapped my arms around Iannis's neck and closed my eyes as he carried me to the bedroom. A few moments later, he set me down on the mattress, and I groaned in relief—it was the softest surface I'd lain on in days. "I am never taking this for granted again," I moaned as Iannis rummaged through a chest of drawers nearby. "Never."

Iannis pulled out a crystal bottle filled with gold liquid and filled two small glasses. "Drink this," he said, handing one to me. "It's a restorative potion for rest and relaxation. I take it when I know I'm only going to manage a couple hours of sleep, and it makes me feel like I've had eight." He downed the contents of his own glass. "We cannot afford the luxury of resting very long, but I'll make it up to you on our honeymoon."

"Sounds good to me." I took a swig, then shimmied out of my clothes and burrowed beneath the blankets with Iannis. As he folded his strong arms around me, I immediately began to drift off. Soon we would be married, and this bed would be *ours*, not just his.

Take that, *Ta'sradala*, I thought sleepily as I drifted off. She might be a bitter old bitch, but Iannis and I were stronger than all the malice in her ancient, blackened heart.

21

The week following our return was a crazy whirlwind of activity. I met Mina, who was very likable and a perfect match for Fenris, and instantly decided to help organize her and Fenris's wedding. It seemed best not to wait, as my shifter senses told me she might already be expecting their first child—or cub, as the case might be. Whichever they got, I had no doubt Fenris would be a wonderful father.

"Why do you think Fenris fell in love now, after going so long without female companionship?" I asked Iannis as we were riding in the carriage to yet another reception. "Do you think he was waiting for Mina all this time?"

"They fit together well," Iannis said, "but I think it just was time for him. When he was a Chief Mage he hid behind his position, duties, and scholarship, and his parents' nagging to find a wife probably had exactly the contrary effect. Then, while he lived here with us, being a fugitive who had to hide his true nature would have been an obstacle. I suppose that being all alone, thrown upon his own resources, made him reevaluate what he truly wanted in life—and lo and behold, there it was, right within reach."

"Very lucky for him," I said, "and for Mina too."

"Now, of course, *our* case is very different," Iannis said. "I was waiting for you, obviously, all those centuries, though without being aware of it. It took me a little while to realize what a treasure had fallen into my lap."

"I forgive you," I said with a wink, planting a kiss on his cheek. "Since you eventually came to your senses."

———

IT WAS a good thing Nelia did most of the actual preparations for Fenris's and Mina's wedding, as I was soon involved in some very unpleasant business. The chief suspect of the aborted Resistance plot, a construction tycoon called Moredo, turned up dead in his cell in the Enforcers Guild. I was called down to investigate whether it had really been suicide, as the enforcers claimed —and even if it was true, why had they left the man his belt to do the deed? That seemed pretty suspicious, and since Iannis was busy with the Convention, the responsibility to find out what had really happened fell on my shoulders.

"Enforcer Baine," Captain Skonel said calmly as I entered his office. His deputy was standing by his side, stiff-backed and stern-faced, but the captain himself seemed relaxed. "I'm happy to see you're back here in one piece."

"As am I." I gave Skonel a smile of my own as I sat down, ignoring the lie. He was certainly *not* happy to see me—I could tell by his change of scent—but he was diplomatic enough not to say so, and since I didn't actually think he wished me dead, I didn't see a need to press the issue. "Do you have the report I asked for?"

"Of course." Skonel gestured to his deputy, who handed me a file. I flipped open the manila folder and perused the contents, which included Moreno's arrest report, notes from several interviews, and the suicide report, which was accompanied by some grisly photographs.

"So," I said slowly, closing the file, "the guards *really* didn't see anything?"

Captain Skonel's expression didn't change. "They'd been checking on him every hour, as instructed," he said. "We don't know how he managed to get hold of the belt he hanged himself with."

"If he didn't have any visitors, then one of the guards must have slipped it to him," I said, pointing out the obvious. "Did you interrogate everyone who was on duty at the time?"

"Of course," Skonel said, a hint of annoyance creeping into his voice. "I know how to do my job."

"Right." I stood up, tucking the file beneath my arm. "I'll need to see the cell, and speak to the guards as well."

Skonel nodded. "My deputy will escort you downstairs."

I held in a snort. Once upon a time, I wouldn't have needed an escort. But times were changing, and though I still had my enforcer license, I was too important to be allowed to wander around without any sort of protection. *Not that I needed help from the likes of the deputy*, I mused as we rode down the rickety elevator. After everything I'd been through recently, I was practically bullet-proof.

I spent the next hour examining the cell and questioning the guards who were on rotation. The cell turned up nothing—there were so many different smells down there it was impossible to isolate which didn't belong—and the guards were equally unhelpful. None of them had seen or done a damn thing, and my nose told me they were truthful. The only idea I could come up with was that an imposter had slipped down here to do the deed...but with no witnesses, it was impossible to pin down who it might have been.

Frustrated, I returned to the captain's office. He looked a little too smug for my taste, clearly happy I hadn't been able to find anything incriminating against his staff.

"What's this Fenris told me about you imprisoning him?" I demanded, determined to find *something* to nail Captain Skonel with. I hid a smug look of my own when he flinched, the reaction barely detectable even to someone with my discerning shifter gaze.

"That was an unfortunate misunderstanding," he said, leaning back in his chair. "One that has been corrected."

"You've got that right." I folded my arms. "How did this 'misunderstanding' arise?"

The captain scowled. "Fenris did not reveal his identity to us," he said. "He was magically disguised, and there was no way for any of us to guess who he truly was until after his illusion failed. Once his identity was revealed, Director Toring vouched for him, and he was released."

"Hmm." I searched his face. "Without your permission, I imagine."

"My permission was irrelevant," the captain said stiffly. "Fenris is not a criminal."

"Damn right he's not." I leaned forward. "How exactly did he come to be in that cell?"

"Enforcer Galid Meltin, from the third crew, brought him in unconscious," Skonel said. "He'd been charged with destroying property and refusing to pay for services at a brothel, though the charges were later discovered to be fraudulent." The captain pressed his lips together. "Once we discovered the deception, we brought in Meltin, who confessed that he arrested Fenris as a favor to a brothel owner, with whom Meltin is close friends. We'll need to look into all his previous bounties from that area." He rummaged in a drawer for a moment and brought out a well-worn leather pouch. "Please return this to Fenris with my apologies that I did not believe him at first. Of course, if he had not tried to disguise himself, this whole thing would not have happened in the first place."

"What's going to happen to Meltin?" I asked, ignoring the captain's excuses. "This seems like an excellent test case for those disciplinary commissions we are setting up."

"True," Skonel admitted grudgingly. "He is in cell eighteen now, and the commission will meet once we have completed the investigation. It turns out that Meltin was not the only rotten apple in the barrel." From the stiffness of his neck, I could tell how much it cost Captain Skonel to admit this. "All of his crew knew what he was up to and turned a blind eye."

I suppressed the urge to say "Told you so" and tucked the pouch in my magic sleeve. "Let me know how things turn out—after my honeymoon." I didn't want to hear about any of this crap until I got back. After dealing with Ta'sradala, I deserved a week or two of peace.

"Very well." Captain Skonel relaxed, and from the change in his scent, I knew he was relieved to have gotten off lightly. "And my best wishes for the forthcoming festivities. I look forward to attending your wedding reception."

———

THE MOST NOTABLE event of that week was Fenris and Mina's wedding—a beautiful ceremony held at Solantha Temple. It was the first time I had seen Fenris in robes, though from his memories, I knew he had worn them every day for most of his long life. Now that he was acknowledged as a mage-shifter hybrid, like me, with magic of his own, he could wear them openly once more, though I had a feeling he'd stick to his tunics as a habit. Mina was absolutely lovely in the wedding gown I'd helped her choose, with those blonde curls and blue eyes, and everyone could tell how much they loved each other as they recited their vows. Her pregnancy was not yet showing but nevertheless lent a special glow to her fair skin. Watching them get married made me look forward even more to my own wedding, which was almost upon us.

After the wedding, we all retreated to the palace for an intimate reception. Since Fenris and Mina didn't want a lot of fuss, and weren't politically prominent, only the close friends and family who'd attended the ceremony were invited.

"Two weddings in one week," Comenius said as he gazed fondly at Rusalia, who was flitting from person to person like an eager butterfly. "It's no wonder she's so excited."

I nodded. "It looks like you're all getting along well these days," I said. Rusalia had made a rough start of it with Comenius and Elania—her mother had just died, and the little girl was rebellious and belligerent. She still had a bit of that wild streak in her, but ever since her near-death experience in the quake, she'd become much more manageable and affectionate.

"Oh, absolutely," Elania agreed. "She is a darling. She has already promised to help look after her little brother and sister, when the time comes." She placed a hand over her belly, which was barely beginning to show.

My eyes widened. "Twins?" I asked in a hushed voice.

She beamed. "We are doubly blessed," she said, planting a kiss on Comenius's cheek.

I hugged them both, feeling absurdly excited for them. "I'm so happy for you both," I said. Everyone seemed to be increasing their families...but Iannis and I would get around to that eventually, when things settled down a bit. *There was no rush*, I told myself.

"You haven't had any more trouble with your in-laws in Manuc?" Com asked, leaning in as he lowered his voice. We'd told Comenius and Elania what had happened, as well as Fenris and Mina, but no one else knew the truth about our long "vacation."

"No, and I don't expect to hear from them again," I said firmly, sincerely hoping I was right.

"Good. They sound far too troublesome."

"If you need any help with them, we are at your service," Elania said.

"I know." I smiled at them, glad that in all likelihood, they would never need to face a Tua. There were some things better left to old legends.

Iannis and I made our rounds through the gathering, talking to Rylan, who complained how boring his life was these days, and to Janta and Tinari, who were doing fine. Tinari had been overcome with joy when I'd returned—when she'd first laid eyes on me, she'd wrapped her arms tight around me and refused to let go for a very long while. Janta informed me that she and the other girls felt guilty, and I'd had to assure them all that what had happened wasn't their fault. Ta'sradala would have found a way to get to me even if I hadn't been playing hide-and-seek in the garden.

Fenris and Mina's friends, Barrla and Marris, a cheerful young couple from Watawis, were playing with Liu, who had got the afternoon off for the occasion. Trouble was observing everything from the curtain rod and occasionally repeating something in his raucous parrot voice.

"We'd love to stay longer," Iannis finally said to Fenris and Mina, who were sitting with Fenris's "grandparents" in the corner, "but unfortunately, Sunaya and I have to be off to the Minister's reception."

"Of course." Mina and Fenris rose. "Thank you so much for doing this for us," Mina said, reaching up so she could hug Iannis. "It is amazing what you two have pulled together on such short notice."

I laughed. "We couldn't have done it without my assistant," I said as I hugged her next. "I'm just glad I got to see the two of you married. You two were made for each other."

"Yes, we are," Fenris said, putting an arm around Mina's shoulder. He kissed the top of her head, and she snuggled into him, her face glowing with pleasure. Exchanging glances, Iannis and I left them to enjoy the rest of their reception, and we changed and got into the carriage.

"We're nearly done with all this wedding business now," I said to Iannis as we slowly progressed through the heavy traffic. "How is the Convention going?" It had kept him very busy, since he was the head of the Canalo delegation and had missed all the preliminary horse-dealing sessions.

"Reasonably well." Iannis smiled. "Yesterday we managed to defeat a new law that the Minister proposed to extend the mandate of Toring's new agency over the entire Federation.

Garrett will still need to work with the Chief Mages, and seek their permission, before he undertakes investigations in our states."

"Garrett won't like that," I said. I could imagine the disappointment on his face when the bill was struck down. "Was there really any chance of something like that getting passed, though? Surely the Chief Mages would not vote for something that decreases their autonomy so much?"

"You'd think so, but it was a near thing. I'm sure they will try again at the next Convention. Toring is nothing if not tenacious."

We arrived at the concert hall and were received by the Minister, as the host. There was some initial tension between him and Iannis that made me wonder if it was just because of the defeated legislation or something more serious—but this wasn't the time to ask Iannis, as both of us were swamped with felicitations, questions, requests, and gossip. The hall was packed with close to a thousand people, including forty-seven of the fifty Chief Mages and many of their families, the entire Federal Government from Dara, the most important foreign diplomats, and the heads of numerous institutions, museums, newspapers, and big companies.

Supposedly, all these bigwigs were there to celebrate Iannis and me getting hitched. It was more likely that they were all here to hobnob and trade favors with each other, but I just went with the flow, chatting with everyone I was introduced to, sipping at my wine, and letting the glitter and noise wash over me like a river. Yes, it was more mind-numbing than filing paperwork, but at least I was back home instead of fighting my way through another one of Ta'sradala's challenges.

As usual, there were a few mages who eyed me with disdain, but I ignored them. I couldn't wait to seal my bond with Iannis, our commitment to each other, in front of the mage community, and finally shut up the naysayers who insisted our romance would never work out. After everything Iannis's grandmother had put me through, I wasn't ever going to let anyone say that I wasn't worthy of Iannis. I had survived those tests for him, and we had made it through the last one together. If that wasn't a sign from the Creator that we were meant to be a couple, I didn't know what was.

22

"*S unaya! Iannis!*"

I froze, mid-conversation with a nosy socialite, at the sound of Fenris's voice in my head. It sounded staticky, like it was coming through a bad radio connection, and I frowned. Was I imagining things?

"Miss Baine?" the socialite asked, giving me an odd look. "Is everything okay?"

I shook off the strange feeling. "Everything's fine," I said. I must have imagined his voice. What would Fenris be doing here anyway? He was supposed to be back at the palace, enjoying his reception with Mina.

"*Sunaya!*" Fenris's voice came through loud and clear this time, blowing *that* theory out of the water. "*Can you hear me?*"

"*Fenris?*" I called back, alarmed now. "*Are you* here?"

"*Outside. I forgot my invitation and the guards won't let us in. We have a theory that the Resistance may have found a way to smuggle in bombs and are planning to blow up the concert hall tonight."*

"Fucking hell," I swore. A possible attack? I'd thought we were past all this!

"Excuse me?" the socialite said, sounding highly offended. I ignored her, stalking away from the crowd so I could duck behind a pillar and take advantage of the relative privacy.

"What's going on?" I asked Fenris, plugging my fingers into my ears to try and drown out the ambient noise.

"This is just a hunch, but Barrla thinks there could be a bomb hidden somewhere inside the concert hall," Fenris said urgently. *"With all the recent construction done on the building, it is entirely possible one could be hidden inside a pillar or behind a wall. We already know for certain that the construction companies are behind the plot—it isn't a stretch to imagine that they rigged this place for the attack."*

"Shit." I bit my lip—the venue owner *had* offered the hall at an absurdly cheap rate, which was why the Minister had chosen to host the reception here. *"We didn't find anything like that during the security check, but I'll speak to Iannis and Garrett immediately. We can't evacuate the place based solely on a hunch, but if we find anything suspicious I'll let you know."*

"Thanks," Fenris said, and then the connection went dead as I moved back into the crowd. Looking around me at the glittering throng, I had to admit that if the Resistance wanted to decapitate the entire mage regime with one fell swoop, tonight would be the ideal occasion. Everyone of power and influence in the Federation was assembled in here, drinking and dancing and

chatting. All the late Benefactor's worst enemies, gathered in one spot.

And yet, from what I gathered, Fenris and his friends merely had a hunch—a suspicion—and no proof whatsoever. I sniffed carefully but could not detect anything amiss, not the slightest whiff of explosives or gunpowder. The vast amount of power concentrated here would easily take care of any attack, unless we were completely blindsided, taken by surprise. Surely the Resistance would know that.

And yet...

Scanning the crowd, I quickly found Garrett standing just a few paces away. I caught his eye, and he moved closer to me at my gesture.

"How carefully did your people vet this venue?" I muttered, leaning in close enough to be heard over the music and buzzing conversation. "Is there any chance you might have overlooked some bomb? Perhaps hidden in the walls or floor?"

He scowled, looking affronted at the very idea. "Sunaya, you know me better than that. We went over everything carefully only this morning, and the guards have been here ever since. Do you really think I would take the slightest risk with the Minister's event? You are perfectly safe—relax and enjoy the party."

"I'm not normally one to be paranoid, but Fenris is outside, and he seems to think there's danger afoot." I briefly explained the theory to Garrett, knowing full well what his answer would be.

"We can't shut this whole place down based on some hair-brained theory," Garrett said firmly. "Like I said, my men and I scoured this place thoroughly. If there was a bomb, we would have found it."

"Right." There was no point in pushing Garrett on this—he was right. But still...my blood was humming now, and I found myself moving toward the entrance. I might as well let Fenris and his friends inside. They could look around while I was stuck here with these politicians.

But when I got to the entrance, Fenris and his party were no longer there, and the majordomo didn't know where they'd gone. The hairs on the back of my neck rose—Fenris wasn't one to give up. If he thought we were truly in danger, he would have found another way to get inside.

"Iannis," I said urgently, striding back inside to where he was standing, deep in some conversation with a Southian diplomat. *"There's something wrong."*

Iannis lifted his head, meeting my gaze across the room. *"What do you mean?"*

"Iannis, are you there?" We both paused at the sound of Fenris's voice, clear as a bell once more. He must be inside, past the wards. *"I need you and Garrett to come down to the basement. We've found an intruder."*

"I'm on my way. Is anyone hurt?"

"No. But come quickly."

"Excuse me," Iannis said to the diplomat as I finally reached him. "Sunaya and I have an urgent matter to attend to." He slipped his arm into mine, and we hurried across the room toward Garrett.

"Come quickly," I said, grabbing his sleeve. He whirled to face me, an annoyed look on his face, and I couldn't blame him—he was in conversation with a stunning brunette who was batting her incredibly long eyelashes at him. "Now."

"Don't tell me you've actually found a bomb," Garrett muttered as he reluctantly allowed me to pull him away.

"I don't know, but Fenris said that he found an intruder in the basement."

"Where are the three of you going off to?" the Minister demanded, planting himself in front of us. He had a plate of canapés in his hand, and was frowning heavily. "This is supposed to be a party in your honor, Iannis."

"I'm afraid this trumps any celebration," Iannis said. "In fact, you'd better come with us, Minister. We have a security issue."

The Minister sputtered, but Iannis steered him toward the basement, explaining the situation as we went. We hurried down the staircase together into a dingy storeroom that looked like a tornado had swept through it. Boxes and party supplies were scattered everywhere, and the far wall had been smashed open. I frowned at the sight of a light switch, which had obviously been covered up by plaster. Was that some sort of trigger?

"Thank the Lady you're here," Fenris said, sounding relieved. His friend Marris was on the ground, straddling a man who had been bound from head to neck with rope. "You're just in time."

"What is the meaning of this?" the Minister demanded, looking at the prisoner and then at the wreckage. "What was this man doing in here?"

"He was paid by the Resistance to come in here and flip that switch," Fenris explained. "He had just uncovered it in the wall when Marris and I caught up to him. It would seem that the whole contraption was arranged while the concert hall was being renovated."

"A walled-in switch?" Garrett echoed. He stalked over to the wall, a scowl on his face. "Damn. These wires could be connected to explosives at any place in the building. It will take some time to trace the wire and disarm whatever trap they're connected to."

"Bloody hell," Iannis swore, echoing my sentiments perfectly. "We need to evacuate the hall at once."

"Yes," Garrett said in a clipped voice. He shook his head, looking absolutely furious. "I can't believe I missed this. We checked this venue *thoroughly*."

"You're not at fault here," I said to Garrett, tactfully deciding not to mention his earlier refusal to look into Fenris's hunch. "You had no reason to tear the walls apart looking for bombs, and stuff like that isn't easily visible. I couldn't even scent anything when Fenris warned me just now. I still don't scent anything suspicious here."

"Let's not stand around here, then," the Minister said impatiently. "The last thing I need is for someone to accidentally trip and hit that switch. Let's get on with it!"

After Garrett ordered two of his agents to guard the switch with their lives, and another pair to take charge of the terrified prisoner, we dispersed. Fenris and Marris explained to me that they'd caught the man who they believed was behind the attack, and I went outside with them to see for myself while everyone else was evacuated. Mina, Barrla, Comenius, and Elania were waiting just beyond the side entrance, along with a group of enforcers.

"Miss Baine." The enforcer in charge inclined his head. "We're ready to transport the prisoner to a holding cell."

"His name is Rubb Slade," Mina explained to me. "I met him at the Solantha Press Club."

"Let me have a look at him," I said. The name didn't at all sound familiar, and I was curious to meet the man who had taken up Thorgana's banner.

Two of the enforcers dragged Rubb forward. He was a thin man with sandy hair and an unpleasant face, and he bared his teeth at me as I leaned in to sniff at him. A familiar scent hit me, and I recoiled in shock.

"By Magorah," I said, looking him up and down again. "You're not Rubb Slade at all. You're Curian Vanderheim, Thorgana's missing husband." He looked completely different, but there was no mistaking the scent. I'd worked Thorgana's parties as a bodyguard enough times to have imprinted her husband's scent in my mind.

"I don't know what you're talking about," the prisoner said stiffly.

"Don't lie to me," I snapped. "You might weigh thirty pounds less and wear a different face, but you stink just like before. You should have hired a mage to change your scent. It's a good thing you're not as bright as your late wife was."

"I knew there was something off about him," Mina cried, her eyes shining with triumph. "Both times I met him he was always talking about how much he hated mages."

"And now we understand why," Fenris said grimly.

"Well, now that we've got all this sorted, why don't you come back with us to the palace?" I said with a grin. "After all, you're a very important person, Mr. Vanderheim. And we certainly wouldn't want you to mysteriously commit suicide in your prison cell, would we?"

Now that the threat had been identified, Iannis and Garrett acted with typical decisiveness. The switch was guarded by Federal Agents, and the guests were evacuated to the palace, where the reception continued. Garrett's people, assisted by enforcer specialists, would work to find out what kind of bomb the switch was connected to, once the wire had been safely cut.

I sighed in relief as Vanderheim was dragged away in manacles, finally realizing how close a shave we'd had that night. If not for Fenris and his friends, all of us could be mangled bodies under the rubble of the concert hall by now. Putting the thought out of my mind, I slung my arms around Mina and Fenris and herded them toward a waiting carriage. I wasn't one to let my enemies ruin my fun, and tonight sure as hell wasn't going to be any different.

Despite our efforts to keep the plot under wraps, the news that they had all just escaped mayhem soon reached the guests, and the party in the palace turned almost wild, with everybody consuming vast quantities of booze to take the edge off the near miss. After a quick council meeting in which everyone gave their reports and we debated how to deal with the aftermath and tighten security measures, Iannis and I joined the guests once more. When the celebration of our survival finally wound down, at nearly two in the morning, we made our way to Iannis's suite at long last only to find an unexpected guest waiting for us in Iannis's sitting room.

"Annia!" I cried as my best friend got to her feet. She looked a bit dusty from the road, in jeans and a red leather jacket. There were circles under her eyes, but the smile on her face was genuine. "You're back!"

"And right on time, too," she said as I wrapped her up in a fierce hug. "I wasn't dressed for that society shindig you had going on out there, and I'm definitely not in the mood for a party after all this travel, but Director Chen was nice enough to let me wait up here for you guys."

"Of course," Iannis said with a warm smile. "You are always welcome in our home."

"I'm so glad to see you," I said, blinking back tears as I pulled back to look at Annia. The exhaustion on her face had worried me initially, but there was a quiet satisfaction in her eyes that made me relax. "I'm guessing you found Noria? Is she okay?"

Annia nodded. "She's on a ship to the Central Continent now," she said. "It was an adventure, tracking her down and getting her on that boat, but at least she'll be safe now." She looked over my shoulder at Iannis. "You're not going to send agents after her, are you? Or punish me for abetting her?"

Iannis shook his head. "So long as she stays on the other side of the pond, she won't hear from me," he said. "With any luck she'll carve a new life for herself and stay out of trouble. I would have pardoned her already if she had shown the least willingness to renounce further subversion. I don't suppose she has seen the error of her ways?"

"She is stubborn as she ever was." Annia sighed. Tears shimmered in her eyes for a moment, but she cleared her throat and blinked them away. "I would have come sooner, but getting all the way back here from the East Coast was a real bitch. I hope you don't mind if I spend the night?"

"'Course not," I said, slapping her on the shoulder. "Besides, that way you and I can get ready for the big day together."

Annia blinked. "Am I still going to be in the wedding?"

I grinned. "I've had your bridesmaid dress ready and waiting for months." She looked a bit leaner than her usual slim self, but Mrs. Lawry, my dressmaker, would quickly take care of any changes needed.

Her face burst into a broad smile. "That's the best news I've heard all week. Where is it? I'd better try it on now and make sure you're not making me look fat!"

Iannis and I exchanged amused glances. "You can always sleep later," he said, laughter in his voice, as he turned to find the familiar flask and glasses. "Here, give some of this to your friend as well. We don't want either of you falling asleep during the ceremony."

"Mmh," Annia said as she drank the potion. "This stuff tastes pretty good. I'm already feeling a nice boost."

"It's too bad you missed the dancing tonight, but the wedding party the day after tomorrow will be even better," I said as I pulled her to my sitting room, where her dress was hanging. "Now that you're back in Solantha, and Noria is safe, are you going to resume working as an enforcer?"

Annia shrugged. "Eventually. It feels kind of strange, catching criminals when my own sister is a fugitive from justice. But maybe something more interesting will turn up."

As she admired the dress, holding it up against her slim figure, Trouble came flitting into the sitting room on noiseless wings and settled on the back of a chair to observe what we were doing in the middle of the night.

"Here, let's see how it fits." Using a few Words, I magicked Annia's travel-worn outfit to the sofa and put the bridesmaid dress on her. Annia slowly turned around, the silk skirt swinging with her movement.

"Prrrettty," Trouble commented, approval in his high-pitched voice. Did he really have an opinion?

"You're gorgeous," I agreed, looking Annia up and down. The

mysterious antique golden choker she never took off sparkled against her skin. "I hope the matching shoes fit, but if not, I can adjust them. My magic is pretty versatile these days."

"So is mine," she said, skimming a hand over the fabric. As I watched, the slight looseness in her waist and bust disappeared, the dress molding itself to her willowy curves like a glove.

I opened my mouth, questions bubbling in my throat, then closed it again. I was curious about her new abilities, which she'd never explained in detail, but could see that despite the potion, she was weary. And if I was honest, I was more eager for my bed than for answers. The questions could wait.

After settling Annia in a comfortable guest room, I stared at Trouble, who had come along companionably. "You, my friend, are clearly able to distinguish a pretty bridesmaid from an ugly one."

"Prretty," he repeated.

"Don't act like you're only capable of parroting. I know better." I squinted, scrutinizing him with magic senses—now heightened and clearer, thanks to the knowledge that I'd absorbed from the Tua. Trouble had been intelligent and able to understand all along, I saw, but was hampered by a limitation I'd set when I first created him, because at the time I was intent on forming merely a stupid, temporary ether pigeon.

"Come here, Trouble."

He squawked, then flapped his wings and soared over to me. As he settled on my left wrist, I caressed his throat with the fingers of my right hand, removing the limitation and strengthening his memory and vitality at the same time.

"Better now?" I asked.

"Much better, Sunaaaya. Thththannkss." I grinned—his pronunciation was still bird-like, but that was the first real, complete sentence he'd ever uttered. He was capable of much more now, and I was looking forward to seeing what else he could do.

But not now, I decided with a yawn. It had been a very long day, and Iannis was waiting for me in our bed.

"Good night, Trouble," I said, stroking him one last time as I headed for the bedroom.

"Good niiight, Sunaaaya."

23

"You're quiet tonight," Iannis said as we sat in the carriage, on our way to yet another reception. "Is everything all right?"

I smiled. "I'm just thinking about how lucky I am to have you," I said, leaning my head against his shoulder.

"As am I to have you," he said, putting his arm around me in a gentle hug. I sighed a little, sinking into him, content to enjoy these quiet few moments while we still could. The reception we were attending tonight had been organized by the ancient Order of Master Mages, which Iannis had joined some five centuries ago. The event was going to be full of powerful mages—arrogant old coots, for the most part—who would no doubt look down their long noses at me because of my youth and lack of mage credentials. A mere apprentice marrying one of their senior members—I could just imagine their acidic comments. But I was determined not to let that spoil my mood. I'd promised myself that I wouldn't be ungrateful for the life I had if I ever got back home, and I wasn't about to break that promise now.

"It's funny," I said as I mused over the events of the past two weeks. "I thought about killing your grandmother more times than I can count while she had me in her clutches, but now that that's all behind me, I almost feel grateful to her."

"Oh?" Iannis lifted an eyebrow quizzically. "And how is that, exactly?"

"Well..." I took a moment to collect my thoughts. "Before she kidnapped me, I was feeling trapped by this new high-society life. All of this schmoozing and planning and dealing with responsibility...it felt like a cage, and like I would never be able to take a free day again and just enjoy life. But being held at Ta's-radala's mercy reminded me of what a cage *really* is, and it's not this. My life with you is a blessing," I said, squeezing Iannis's hand. "This whole ordeal has really put things in perspective for me."

Iannis smiled. "Does that mean that the lady mages in attendance tonight do not have to fear for their clothing?" he teased.

"I'm not so sure about that." I stuck out my tongue. "I know finally tying the knot will help, but it's still going to take a lot of discipline to ignore all the naysayers. Especially after I've gone up against a Tua. I doubt any of these mages have even *seen* one, never mind gone up against one."

Iannis nodded. "Now that Fenris has officially been pardoned and is safe"—Iannis had blackmailed the Minister into issuing that pardon by using an old but dangerous secret against him

—"there is no more need to hide the extent of your magical knowledge. Perhaps we should just end your apprenticeship now, and be done with all that. I too am getting tired of all the criticism and negativity, especially since I know better than anyone else how woefully they underestimate you."

I raised an eyebrow. "Does that mean I have your blessing to rattle some cages tonight?" My brain immediately began to conjure various possibilities...scenes I'd fantasized about during past moments of frustration.

Iannis chuckled. "I wouldn't exactly say that," he said as we pulled up in front of the manor gates. "But if the situation warrants it, I certainly don't want to stop you. The last thing I want is for you to become some boring society matron."

I laughed as the carriage door opened. "I can assure you," I said to Iannis as I took the footman's hand and let him help me out, "there is absolutely zero chance of *that* happening."

———

IANNIS and I entered the manor arm in arm and were immediately greeted by Balthur ar'Zaronian, the Grand Master of the Order of Master Mages. He was a tall, regal man in deep purple and grey robes that set off his shining silver beard and long hair. His hair was tied back in a low tail, much like Iannis wore his.

"I am very pleased that you could make it, Lord Iannis," he said enthusiastically. "The way I hear it, the Mages Guild was uncertain as to whether you would make it back in time for your own wedding!"

"Yes, we had some unexpected business come up at the last minute," Iannis said smoothly. We'd agreed not to talk much about the Tua connection for now, or the true nature of our travels. "This is my bride-to-be, Sunaya."

"As lovely as your pictures in the paper," the old mage said, bowing over my hand. I was relieved to see no derision or malice in his eyes—if this man thought I was unworthy of my position, he at least had the good sense to hide it. "Iannis has told me much about you in his letters. I hear that you are already powerful, and will be formidable when fully trained. How is your apprenticeship coming along?"

"Pretty well," I said, smiling. If only he knew...

We chatted with the Grand Master for a little while, then circulated amongst the rest of the crowd. Grand Masters from several continents were among the guests—two thirds of them male, and all well past their first century. Their interests focused on magic rather than politics, and several conversed with one another in Loranian on esoteric subjects. Even without knowing their backgrounds, I could have guessed that these mages were of a higher caliber than at the other receptions—the air was practically humming with power.

Many of the guests seemed skeptical of me, but they made efforts to be polite, even as they subtly tested my knowledge. I surprised quite a few of them with my grasp of magical theory and fluency in Loranian, thanks to Fenris's broad knowledge. At the end of each little tête-à-tête, I felt a little more confident. They might be learned and accomplished, but I could hold my own.

"Just look at her," a thin, elderly mage sneered under his breath as I passed. "Strutting about as if she owns the place. She is a mere apprentice—if not for her husband-to-be, she would not even be allowed amongst us."

"What was that?" I asked sweetly, turning on my heel. The mage's face paled—no doubt he'd thought he was out of earshot, unaware of my sharp shifter hearing.

He set his jaw and met my gaze squarely. "I see no need to repeat myself," he said as the room quieted around us.

"No, of course not," I said softly. "You're too much of a coward to say that again to my face, now that the entire room can hear you. But if you really think I don't belong amongst you," I added, raising my voice so that everyone else could hear, "then how about a little challenge?"

"You're not strong enough to challenge any one of us," he scoffed. "We do not measure ourselves against mere children."

"Then you should have no problem accepting," I said with a smirk. "Let's see who can levitate the largest amount of people in this room. I bet you can do, oh, ten?"

"Ten! Don't make me laugh," he spat, raising his arms. As he did, several of the guests began to gasp as they were slowly lifted into the air. Raising an eyebrow, I looked around the vast ballroom and counted.

"Fifteen, sixteen, seventeen, eighteen, nineteen..." I trailed off to look at him—beads of sweat had gathered at his temple, and his cheeks were red with exertion. "Twenty."

His breath came out in a whoosh, and the guests landed on the ground in a heap. "That wasn't very gracious of you," I said as the unwitting participants got to their feet, cries of outrage echoing throughout the room.

"As if I care what you think," he panted, trying to look righteous. "I did far more than ten—I doubled that number."

"How nice for you," I cooed, lifting my own arms. The guests cried out in alarm as their feet began to lift off the floor—all four hundred-ish of them, including my challenger. I left Iannis and the Grand Master on the ground out of respect, but sent the rest of them soaring high up, until their heads were nearly touching the ceiling. From below, it was a funny sight—all those feet and shoes dangling in the air. Lucky for them, the robes hid their underwear pretty well.

Finally, when I felt my magic begin to strain under the weight, I gently lowered them back down to the ground. As their feet touched the tiled floor, a hush fell over the room. I met the old mage's flabbergasted stare as they all gaped at me, many with their jaws nearly to the floor. With the exception of Iannis, and maybe a few of the Grand Masters, none of them would have been able to carry this off without losing control.

"That was stupendous!" our host cried, striding forward. "My dear, I would never have guessed you capable of such a feat. And I confirmed that it was all your own doing—Iannis was simply standing by. How in Recca did you manage it?"

"When Iannis and I went to Manuc, I was sent on a training mission to the Tua realm," I said nonchalantly, as if I were talking about the weather. "Time passes much faster in there, and during the week that passed in our world, I absorbed years of top-notch training that can't be received anywhere else." That last bit was true enough—there were definitely things in the knowledge Alara and Nalan had given me that humans didn't know.

Astonished murmurs swept through the crowd at that news.

"The *Tua*?"

"I thought they were just an old legend."

"I guess it has to be true, after what she just did."

And on it went. Many of the mages looked at me with newfound respect. I struggled not to laugh at the confounded expressions on their faces.

"Well, that would explain your unusual mastery, though the strength you exhibited is just as extraordinary," the Grand Master said. "I've never seen a first-year apprentice exert so much control over her magic." Though he didn't say it aloud, his scent told me he was still a bit dubious of my sensational claim.

"Indeed," Iannis said, sliding an arm around my waist. "Sunaya will be taking the graduation exam as soon as we return from our honeymoon. As you have all witnessed, she is one of the strongest mages in the entire Federation, ready to claim her robes. She has learned some things, like the Tua language, that were new even to me."

"Congratulations," the Grand Master said, snagging a glass of champagne from a nearby waiter and pressing it into my hand.

"Let us toast to you now, Sunaya—to the end of your apprentice-ship, and the beginning of what is sure to be a glorious and fruitful magical career!"

"I can certainly drink to that," I said, lifting my glass to him. I drained my drink as everyone else in the room did the same, doing my best to hide the grin on my face. I knew better than to think I'd won over every mage in the room, but I'd managed to impress the Grand Master, and that sure as hell was good enough for me.

24

"By the Ur-God," Annia exclaimed as our six-horse carriage drew to a halt. "How the hell have I never known this temple was here? It's not exactly tiny."

I grinned, the ball of nerves in my stomach lessening in the face of Annia's awe. "It's a closely guarded secret amongst mages," I said as she stared at Solantha Temple, which had just shimmered into view. Inside, hundreds of mages from all over the Northia Federation were waiting to witness the wedding of the decade—the scandalous wedding of a Chief Mage and a shifter hybrid.

And amongst them were my closest friends.

"Don't worry," Rylan called to Annia as he slipped out of one of the temple's side doors. His eyes sparkled as he looked her up and down, admiring her outfit. "I had the same reaction when I first saw the place. Best kept secret in Solantha, eh?" He winked at me.

"And good morning to you too," I said, my lips twitching as he offered me his arm. "You ready to give me away?" Rylan was the oldest male in my immediate family, so the duty fell to him despite the fact that he was so close in age to me.

"I was born ready," my cousin said, leaning in to peck my cheek. "You look stunning, cousin. Classy and sexy at the same time, with all that black lace. You're going to knock their socks off in that dress."

Grinning, I looked down at myself one last time. The seamstress had been furious when she'd learned I'd lost even *more* weight during my time away, and I'd promised her I would gain it back in time for the wedding. Luckily, I'd been able to keep my word —I filled the gown out nicely, and she'd only had to take it in half an inch at the waist. Gaining back ten pounds in a week was no mean feat, but Cook had helped me out in that regard, serving all my favorite dishes day after day.

But in the end, appearances were unimportant. I was about to give my solemn, irrevocable pledge to the love of my life, and receive his in turn. *That* was important, not the dress, or the number and importance of our guests. Inside that gleaming temple, Iannis was waiting for me.

"I'll go on ahead," Annia said, smiling at me. She gave me a quick hug. "You've got this, Sunaya."

I nodded, drawing in a deep breath through my nose as I watched Annia disappear through the doors. The scent of dew-covered grass and late-blooming flowers filled my lungs, calming me a little. Iannis and I had decided on an early morning wedding—to start our life together as husband and wife with the dawning sun, which was cresting over the horizon even now, painting the sky in gorgeous shades of gold and pink.

"Come on, hot stuff," Rylan said, nudging me a little. "Let's get you hitched."

I tightened my grip on Rylan's arm as we slowly walked through the doors and into the temple's packed interior. All eyes turned toward me, and I straightened my spine and held my head high, gliding across the runner as if I had all the time in the world. So much attention was a little nerve-wracking, but I was determined not to show it. I was thankful that at least no journalists or cameras were allowed in this sacred place.

The wedding party was waiting ahead, directly in front of Resinah's statue—Fenris stood proudly at Iannis's side, and Annia was waiting for me near the priest's elbow, looking gorgeous in the deep green sheath gown I'd commissioned for her. Iannis was dashingly handsome in his ivory wedding robes, his long hair falling loose around his shoulders. His eyes shone with loving pride as our gazes met across the aisle.

My own heart was in my throat as I finally reached the appointed space and Rylan handed me off to Iannis. I gripped his hand tightly as we turned to face the priest, and Iannis gave me a reassuring squeeze.

"You look good enough to eat," he said in mindspeak. *"I hope you've come prepared for a feast after this."*

I choked back a laugh at the blatant innuendo in his tone, and my nerves immediately evaporated. *"Maybe I'll eat you first,"* I suggested, resisting the urge to stick my tongue out at him.

"I wouldn't object to that in the slightest."

"Family and friends of the bride and groom," the priest intoned, his voice echoing through the dome as he addressed the crowd. "Welcome to Solantha Temple, where we have gathered today to witness the joining of these two souls in holy and eternal matrimony. In this sacred place, before the Creator and the First Mage, we are privileged to share this unique moment in the lives of Iannis and Sunaya, where the two finally become one."

"Though you may not have known each other your entire lives," he said, turning to address us next, "you have nevertheless been gravitating toward this day since you were born, and your union will last as long as you both shall live. As is our ancient custom, you pledge yourselves to each other and move forward into the future as one. Before you declare your vows, I want to hear you confirm that it is indeed your intention to marry today."

"Sunaya, do you come here today, freely and of your own will, to give yourself to Iannis in marriage?"

"I do," I managed to say over the swell of emotion in my throat. By Magorah, this was really happening. We were finally here together, beneath the eyes of the Creator and Resinah and whoever else was looking down at us. I wondered if my mother could see me now, and I blinked back tears at the thought of her. I hoped she would be proud of me today.

"Very good. And Iannis, do you too come here today, freely and of your own will, to give yourself to Sunaya in marriage?"

"I do," Iannis said solemnly.

"Very good." The priest smiled at us. "Iannis and Sunaya, now that you have declared your intentions to marry, please face each other and hold hands so that you may declare your marriage vows."

Iannis and I turned toward each other, and my heart flipped over in my chest as he smiled broadly at me. "I, Iannis," he said, reciting the vows we'd spent weeks agonizing over, "bind myself to you forevermore as your loving husband. I promise to spend each day working to become the truest version of myself, for you, for us, and for our family. I vow to stand by your side throughout the rest of our long lives—to warm you on cold winter mornings, to watch our love grow during the soft days of spring, to work and play hard together in the light of the summer sun, and to hold you close in the days of autumn, when the leaves fall and we begin to look toward yet another year together. I will love you for all of our days together, and cherish you above all others in my life."

"Dammit," I sniffled, swiping at the tears running down my face. I'd told myself I wasn't going to cry, but my vision blurred, and my heart swelled so big in my chest that I thought I was going to burst. Thankfully, I wasn't the only one—I could hear other people sniffling too.

The priest conjured a handkerchief, and I carefully dabbed at my eyes. Somehow, I managed to get the words of my own vow out without my voice breaking, gripping Iannis's hands tightly the entire time.

"I, Sunaya," I said in a clear voice that only trembled a little, "promise to live with you for the rest of our lives, as your loving wife. I shall strive to honor our union with steadfastness, truth, and courage. I look forward to spending the seasons of life at your side, as your equal, best friend, and, I hope, the mother of our future children, in good times or bad, wealth or adversity. I will love you for all of our days together, and cherish you above all others in my life."

His steady gaze kept me grounded, and by the time I got out the last of it, I was calm again. I hadn't expected this occasion to be quite this emotional, but I'd gotten through it. I'd committed, and to my surprise, all I felt was relief and happiness. This was a responsibility I accepted with no reservations, no second-guessing.

"Now that the two of you have exchanged your vows, it is time to seal this pact with the marriage spell," the priest announced when I was done. "Best man, bridesmaid, do you have the rings?"

"Yes," Annia and Fenris said, coming forward. They handed us the white gold bands, which we carefully slipped onto each other's ring fingers before turning to face the priest again. He took our joined hands gently in his, then began to chant the Loranian marriage spell that would bind us forever. His sonorous voice echoed through the chamber, and my skin began to tingle as the air around us buzzed with power. I'd seen Fenris and Mina go through the same thing just a few days ago at their own wedding, but I had no idea it was so powerful—it felt like a live electric current was running through me. Did this happen at all mage weddings?

Suddenly, a flood of emotion swept through me, so brilliant and intense that I had to grip Iannis's hand tighter to steady myself. I felt Iannis tense next to me as an invisible bond snapped between us, and I sucked in a sharp breath as all of Iannis's feelings—the joy, the pride, the sharp edge of relief—crashed into me. I turned toward him, and his wide-eyed expression told me he was feeling the same thing from me. The bond that had been forged between us with the serapha charm was now strengthened a hundredfold.

"And so, it is done," the priest said. He released our hands, smiling broadly at us. "You may now kiss your bride, Lord Iannis."

Before I could blink, Iannis crushed me against his chest and kissed me deeply. Cheers and clapping filled the inside of the temple as I wrapped my arms around him and kissed him back, savoring the tender, passionate feelings that passed between us. I could hardly believe this was real, but as his arms tightened around me, and the seconds drew out as we kissed beneath Resinah's benevolent gaze, I began to accept that it was.

I wonder if Resinah really was a special Tua who loved humans and came here to share her gifts with them, I thought. All those clues had to mean something...but did it truly matter? Her wisdom and affection for us spoke for themselves, whatever her origins.

Resinah laughed softly in my head as Iannis finally pulled back. A sense of knowing came over me—there was some connection, but the truth about her origins was more complicated and mysterious than I had imagined. I was glad I hadn't discussed the Tua's suggestion with anyone—there was no point in bringing it up and confusing everyone. Let things stand as they were.

"My blessings on your union," Resinah's voice echoed in my mind, and from Iannis's startled expression, I knew he'd heard it too. *"May you both live a long and happy life as one."*

Iannis and I both bowed our heads and silently thanked her. Joy swept through us both as we turned to face the crowd—there was no greater honor than being blessed by the Lady, except perhaps from the Creator himself.

"We did it," Iannis said as the crowd clapped and cheered. *"We are finally husband and wife."*

"We sure are," I said, grinning at our friends, who were sitting up at the front row and waving furiously at us. *"Now why don't we go and enjoy that feast?"*

———

AFTER THE WEDDING, everyone returned to Solantha Palace for the public reception, where we'd be on full display for the rest of the world. As soon as we alighted from our decked-out horse-drawn carriage—following a human and shifter custom, I'd insisted on hanging a sign from the back that read "JUST MARRIED"—I was nearly blinded by the multiple flashes of light from the waiting paparazzi. Iannis and I were whisked away by security and taken to the back garden, where we spent nearly an hour taking more photographs with the palace's official photographer.

The first half hour was just me and Iannis, but Fenris, Annia, Rylan, and my Aunt Mafiela were brought in for the last half. When we'd planned the wedding, I had been unsure whether this photo session was truly necessary. I would never forget my wedding anyway, and so much posing seemed an excessive display of vanity. However, Nelia and Aunt Mafiela had convinced me that my wedding was not just important for Iannis and me—our union was being watched by shifters and humans throughout the Federation and beyond. Let them see how radiant and happy a shifter and mage pairing could be, they had argued. Our example might help the next unorthodox couple. Besides, our children, and theirs, might like to see how we had celebrated today. So I forced myself to be patient, and posed as required.

"You look wonderful in that gown, Sunaya," Aunt Mafiela said afterward, taking me by the shoulders and looking me up and down. "It is just your style."

"Thank you." I smiled, trying not to roll my eyes. The way she was swelling with pride, as if I were her daughter, you never would have guessed that just last year, she and I had been at each other's throats, driven to hatred by twelve years of bitterness between us. "I'm glad you came," I said, and I meant it. I was very happy that those terrible years were behind us.

"Yeah, you're a real fancy pants now, *Lady Sunaya,*" Rylan teased, cuffing me on the shoulder. "Guess I won't be able to mess around with you anymore, now that you're the wife of such an important guy." He waggled his brows at Iannis, who simply chuckled.

This time I did roll my eyes, and punched Rylan in the shoulder for good measure. "Just you wait," I said as Iannis put an arm around my waist and began to gently lead me toward the palace. "I'll kick your ass the next time we're on the mat together, Rylan. Lady or not."

Rylan's laughter followed us into the ballroom, where we made a glorious entrance. The place was packed with nearly a thousand guests, and they all toasted us as one. Fenris and Annia made grand speeches, making the audience laugh as they recounted anecdotes about us, and nearly making me cry all over again when they praised us.

"You are, and always will be, the kindest, bravest, and most ferocious soul I've ever known," Annia said, her cheeks pink as her eyes shone brightly with love and pride. "And you," she said, turning to Iannis. "I wasn't sure about you when we first met, but I've learned from working with you that you're smart as hell, compassionate, and you've got a spine of steel under those robes. I can't think of a more perfect match for my best friend."

The crowd cheered again, and with that, we broke off to feast and mingle. We spent the first hour receiving endless congratulations from the guests, including Annia's mother. I hadn't been certain she would come, but not only had she shown up, she was even talking to Annia again, and the two looked like they were getting along. I wondered if Annia had told her that she'd found Noria and gotten her to safety. The golden collar around Annia's neck gleamed, and I wondered just how much she'd come to rely on that spirit within. Her skin glowed with a soft, almost ethereal light that I hadn't noticed before.

"One of these days," Iannis murmured, noticing where I was staring, "we will get that story out of her. But tonight, we should look toward the future, not the past."

Later, I sat with Fenris while Iannis was talking to Mina. "Thank you for staying on, saving us the other night, and standing with us on this day," I said, smiling up at him. He should be on his honeymoon himself, but he and Mina had decided to stay until after our wedding, since Fenris was Iannis's best man. "How do you feel, now that you're a married man?"

"Like I am finally complete." Fenris gave me a broad smile. "I never knew what I was missing before meeting Mina. I only hope you and Iannis are half as happy...but I am sure you are. It was clear to everyone during the ceremony earlier that, despite all differences, you belong together."

"Duh." I stuck my tongue out at him. "I'm glad everyone is finally getting with the program."

Fenris laughed. "Of course, *I* knew this much earlier—before the two of you had an inkling," he teased.

We sat in contented silence for a while, happy to just enjoy each other's company after being separated for so long. "I'm so glad you are no longer under threat, after that pardon for Polar ar'Tollis," I said softly, pitching my voice so nobody could hear. "Pretending to be your own son was all well and good, but now you're truly safe."

"It is quite a relief," he admitted. "Though I had adjusted to living under the threat of execution, now that I'm married, and hoping to be a father soon, it is better not having to dodge the authorities or use multiple false names."

"Sunaya," a familiar voice called. I spun around in shock to see that Deryna was behind us, with Drawe standing shyly by her side. "Congratulations on your marriage," she said, smiling fondly at us. "I am so glad that you two pulled through. There were times when I despaired of a happy outcome, but I prayed that the Creator would help you escape."

"Thank you, Aunt Deryna," Iannis said as I tried to find my voice. He didn't seem the least bit surprised to see them. "I very much appreciate you two coming out."

"Is Ennartha here, too?" I asked in a hushed voice. "And...and..." I couldn't bring myself to pronounce that wicked woman's name, and desperately hoped she hadn't set foot in the Federation.

"No, don't worry," Deryna said, correctly interpreting my expression. "Ennartha sends her regards, but she never visits Northia, not even for this, any more than her mother would. And speaking of Ta'sradala"—she grinned, an expression that made her look significantly younger—"the scuttlebutt is that Ta's-radala has incurred the serious displeasure of the High King for sending you to their realm, and has been forbidden to visit Earth for the next five hundred years. I understand she hasn't taken it well."

"Five hundred years?" Iannis and I said at the same time, sounding stunned. We exchanged looks of absolute delight. "You could not have brought us a better wedding present," I said fervently, and Deryna laughed. Ta'sradala had gotten off lightly, in my opinion, but by the time she was allowed to come back to Recca, our children would be grown. And that was no small comfort.

"And how are you, Drawe?" Iannis asked, crouching down to meet the boy's eyes. "Are you enjoying your time in Solantha?"

"It's so big," he said in a hushed voice, his eyes wide. His gaze darted around the room before going back to Iannis. "I've never seen so many people in my life."

"I'm really happy you could make it out," I said, hugging Deryna and Drawe. "You two were kind to me when I was alone and friendless, and I will never forget that. But how did you get here so fast?"

Deryna smiled, pulling a gulaya out of her pocket. "My wonderful nephew sent me this," she said, patting Iannis on the arm. "We arrived just yesterday."

"Keeping secrets, are we?" I asked Iannis, arching a brow at him.

He only smiled. "I thought it would be a nice surprise."

"And so it is," I said, smiling at them all. "I'm guessing you're staying here at the palace?"

"We are."

"Good. Then make sure you find Liu, Tinari, and Rusalia," I told Drawe. "They're the friends I was telling you about who live here. Tell the librarian, Janta Urama, that I sent you, and she'll put you in touch. Iannis and I are going on our honeymoon, but you guys can stay here as long as you like. I hope you'll have a great time."

"We are planning on staying here for a few weeks before returning," Deryna said. "I wish you two a lovely honeymoon. You certainly deserve it after everything you've been through."

"And now," Director Chen, who was acting as tonight's master of ceremonies, called in a magically enhanced voice as the chatter quieted down, "it is time for the bride and groom to open the first dance."

Iannis and I looked at each other. "Are you ready?" he asked, offering his hand.

I smiled, wordlessly slipping my hand in his. The crowd parted as a slow, beautiful melody started up and Iannis gracefully led me onto the empty dance floor. The world fell away as I looked into his eyes, and as we swirled and glided across the room, volumes seemed to pass between us without either of us saying a word. After the first minute or so, other couples joined in, and soon we were at the center of a happy throng. Rylan was swinging Annia around with great energy, and Com was smiling at Elania as they danced. Fenris and Mina were pretty lively on the floor together, I noticed with approval. It was like we were all one big, happy family.

The song was just winding down when something odd flickered at the limits of my vision. Frowning, I looked over Iannis's shoulder at the ballroom and activated my mage sight.

"What is it?" Iannis asked, sensing my tension.

"It seems that Deryna and Drawe aren't our only unexpected guests," I murmured. "Nalan and Alara are standing by those pillars behind you."

I looked at the Tua twins directly, and they both smiled and waved. They had glamored themselves to look human, but beneath the magic, they were just as gigantic as they had been in the Tua realm. As I stared, Broghan popped out from behind Alara and soared across the room in baby dragon form. The guests gasped as he let out a thin stream of flame, forming a heart that blazed directly above us.

"What a charming illusion," I heard somebody gush. "It will soon be the rage at every wedding, I'd bet."

"We have come to learn more of the human world," Broghan said to me in mindspeak as he did a few somersaults. He was stealing the show, but he was way too cute for me to care. *"My father has given his permission, as long as my cousins accompany me."*

"Do you think you might act as a guide for us?" Alara asked. *"Once you come back from your honeymoon, of course."*

"We have a number of experiments we'd like to perform," Nalan added, *"and could use a native guide to help us minimize the damage."*

I held back a snort. *"I'll think about it,"* I told them, then relayed what they'd said to me to Iannis in mindspeak. *"I'm kind of torn,"* I told Iannis as the song came to an end. *"On the one hand, I don't love the idea of them running around doing 'experiments' in our world, but I shudder to think of what havoc they could wreak unsupervised."* Not that I had a chance to control even one of them, but hopefully they would listen to their expert in local culture. They had all my memories, but would they be able to make proper sense of them? Did they have a true idea just how vulnerable Recca's people were when faced with the might of the Tua?

"The mind boggles at the possibilities," Iannis said, though he did not sound too worried.

Inspired, I flagged down Rylan and Annia, who were still together on the dance floor. "You complained that your life was too boring," I told my cousin with an evil grin. "I have just the remedy for that. You and Annia are going to look after some foreign guests while I'm gone."

They glanced at each other. "I happen to be at loose ends," Annia said, shrugging. "Why not?"

"What's the catch?" Rylan asked suspiciously.

"Just that they'll keep you on your toes," I said airily. "You get to babysit someone far smarter and more powerful than you, which will be excellent practice for whatever you choose to do afterwards. If you can get through this, you can do anything."

"Gee, thanks," Rylan said sarcastically, but Annia looked intrigued. I wondered just how powerful that amulet had made her, and if she could hold her own against Broghan. Amused, I lost no time introducing Rylan and Annia to our interdimensional tourists. They were all eyeing one another curiously and getting acquainted when Iannis pulled me away for one last dance.

"That's some challenge you set Rylan and Annia," he commented.

"But in our absence, the best you could do. Let's not worry about what happens until we get back."

"Right. With any luck, Solantha will still be standing."

When the dance ended, we turned to face the crowd as one, and Iannis wrapped his hand in mine. "Thank you all for celebrating with us," he said to the crowd. "Sunaya and I are off to our honeymoon now. Please enjoy the festivities, and drink to our good health while we are gone!"

He pulled out a gulaya from his sleeve and activated it amongst cries of protest from the crowd. The last thing I saw was Director Chen and Fenris's knowing smiles as we disappeared, and the next thing I knew, we were standing on a sandy beach, looking out at a spectacular sunset. I felt a momentary queasiness, but it quickly passed.

"Holy shit," I said, looking around. Chills ran up and down my spine as I took in the familiar surroundings. "This is the island where we first made love, isn't it?"

"Indeed," Iannis said, scooping me up. He carried me up the beach to where a charming seaside cottage sat, its white stone walls sparkling in the dying sun. "I bought it in your name and had a few improvements made," he said as he waved the front door open with a bit of magic.

"I can see that," I said as he carried me inside. I craned my neck, trying to get a good look at the small but cozy space. Everything was done in shades of blue and white, and the smell of salt and verbena and fresh paint permeated the air. "Are you going to give me a tour?"

"Maybe later," he said, setting me atop the bed. He made my clothes vanish with the snap of a finger as he crawled on top of me. "For now, I believe you promised me a feast," he said, a wicked glint in his eye.

I let Iannis cover my naked body with his own, savoring the feel of his warm skin and hard muscles against me as he kissed me deeply. His scent seeped into my very pores, and I took in a deep breath as I wrapped my arms tightly around him, deliriously happy at the thought that this man was finally mine. I could feel his raging lust and passion as his tongue tangled with mine, as he skimmed his hands down my curves lovingly.

But just as he was about to slip his hand between my legs, I flipped us over and straddled him on the bed. "What do you think you're doing?" he asked a bit breathlessly, though the grin on his face told me he knew exactly what I was about.

"Remember," I said as I slid down his body to take him in my hands. "I promised that I would feast on you first."

And so I did, until Iannis finally yanked me away from him, then pinned me to the bed and sank himself deep inside me. As the orgasm took me, a ferocious wave of pleasure that had me crying out his name and tearing the bedsheets with my nails, I imprinted the memory into my mind forever.

No matter what happened next, I would always have this. Our first night together as husband and wife, and many more to come after. It had been a long, bumpy ride to get to this point, but I wouldn't trade any of it for the world.

We finally had our happily ever after.

THE END

Sunaya's adventure may be over...but Jasmine is still writing books! Click the link below to check out Dragon's Gift, the first book in her latest fantasy series!

FIND DRAGON'S GIFT ON AMAZON

GLOSSARY

Annia: see under Melcott, Annia.

Apprenticeship: all mages are expected to complete an apprenticeship with some master mage, that usually lasts from age fifteen to about twenty-five. Only after the final exam may they use colorful robes, and are considered legally of age. Sunaya started her apprenticeship at age 24, under Chief Mage Iannis ar'Sannin, when her magic was first discovered.

ar': suffix in some mages' family names, that denotes they are of noble birth, and can trace their descent to one of Resinah's twelve disciples.

Baine, Mafiela: Chieftain of the Jaguar Clan and Sunaya's aunt. They were estranged after Mafiela threw Sunaya out onto the streets at age twelve, but have since reconciled.

Baine, Melantha: Sunaya's cousin and Rylan's sister, eldest daughter to the Jaguar Clan's Chieftain Mafiela Baine.

Baine, Rylan: Sunaya Baine's cousin, and like her, a panther shifter. He was an active member of the Resistance, with the rank of Captain, he was captured and imprisoned during the uprising in Solantha, and worked off part of his sentence as Sunaya's bodyguard. He was pardoned in recognition of his rescue work during the big quake.

Baine, Sunaya: a half-panther shifter, half-mage who used to hate mages and has a passion for justice. Because magic is forbidden to all but the mage families, Sunaya was forced to keep her abilities a secret until she accidentally used them to defend herself in front of witnesses. Rather than condemn her to death, the Chief Mage, Iannis ar'Sannin, chose to take her on as his apprentice, and eventually his fiancée. Their wedding will be very grand, and is rapidly approaching.

Barrla, see under Kelling, Barrla.

Benefactor: the anonymous, principal source of financial support to the Resistance, who was eventually unmasked as the socialite Thorgana Mills (now deceased).

Canalo: one of the fifty states making up the Northia Federation, located on the West Coast of the Northia Continent.

Castalis: a country and peninsula at the southwestern edge of the Central Continent, ruled by a High Mage who is related to Sunaya, though he cannot publicly acknowledge it.

Central Continent: the largest of the continents on Recca, spanning from Garai in the east to Castalis in the west.

Chen, Lalia: the current Director of the Canalo Mages Guild in

Solantha. She immigrated to the Northia Federation from Garai after her apprenticeship, and serves as deputy to Iannis ar'Sannin, the Chief Mage.

Chief Mage: ruler of one of the fifty states of the Northia Federation, usually addressed as "Lord Firstname". The Chief Mages come together as the Convention every other year to enact legislation, usually in the capital Dara.

Chieftain: a title used to distinguish the head of a shifter clan.

Comenius: see Genhard, Comenius.

Convention: the assembly of all Chief Mages and highest authority in the Federation, source of all Federal legislation. It usually meets every other year in the capital Dara, but sometimes convenes more frequently, or in other locations.

Creator: the ultimate deity, worshipped by all three races under different names.

Croialis: a poison made from the seed of a tropical plant, popular for assassinations as it is not susceptible to magical healing.

Dara: capital of the Northia Federation, located on the east coast of the Northia Continent.

Dira: Lord Iannis's principal secretary in the Mages Guild offices in Solantha.

Dolan, Marris: a young farmer from Abbsville in the state of Watawis, who has spent some time fighting for the Resistance.

Friend and neighbor to Fenris, with whom he came to Solantha to uncover the Resistance Plot there.

Downtown: the seamy area of Maintown, especially at night, when the Black Market is operating there. Full of brothels and gaming dens.

Elania Tarrignal: wife of Comenius Genhard; a witch specializing in potions, with a shop in Witches' End, The Black Curtain.

Elnos: see under Ragga, Elnos.

Enforcer: a bounty hunter employed by the government to seek out and capture wanted criminals. They operate under strict rules and are traditionally paid bounties for each head, although Sunaya is trying to reform this system. While the majority of them are human, there is a strong minority of shifters, and even the occasional mage.

Enforcers' Guild: the administrative organization in charge of the enforcers, currently led by Captain Wellmore Skonel. Also, the building from which the various enforcer crews work under their respective foremen.

Faricia: a large continent that straddles the North and South hemispheres, located south of the Central Continent's western region. Inhabited by many different nations and tribes; partly inaccessible to foreign travelers.

Federation: see Northia Federation.

Fenris aka "Jalen Fenris Shelton," originally Polar ar'Tollis: a clanless wolf shifter who used to be a mage before his illegal transformation; close friend and confidant of Chief Mage Iannis ar'Sannin and Sunaya Baine. After transferring his entire memories and knowledge to Sunaya to save her life, he disappeared from Solantha during the big quake, and was thought dead for a time. In fact, he moved to a small rural community to avoid the scrutiny of the Federal authorities, where he met and became engaged to Mina, a young mage and veterinarian.

First Mage: see under Resinah.

Firegate Bridge: Solantha's best-known structure, a large red bridge spanning the length of Solantha Bay. It is accessible via **Firegate Road**, adjacent to **Firegate Park**.

Garai: the largest and most populated country on the Eastern Continent. Garaians are known for slanted eyes and ivory skin as well as their complicated, rune-like alphabet. Sunaya and Iannis travelled there as part of an official delegation for the Mage-Emperor's funeral and his successor's coronation.

Genhard, Comenius: a hedgewitch from Pernia, owner of the shop **Over the Hedge** at Witches' End. Close friend of Sunaya Baine, father of Rusalia Genhard, former employer of Noria Melcott, and husband of the witch Elania.

Genhard, Rusalia: daughter of Comenius Genhard. She came from Pernia to Solantha to live with her father after her mother's sudden death, and at first had some trouble adjusting, and controlling her fire magic.

Graning, Zavian: mage, currently Minister of the Northia Federation. Elected by the Convention for an indefinite term, he is charged with coordination of governmental business and particularly foreign affairs, between the biannual Convention sessions that he prepares and presides.

Great Accord: a treaty struck by the ruling mages centuries ago, which brought an end to a devastating war known as the Conflict. It is still the basis upon which mages rule their countries and territories. All new laws passed must be in accordance with the provisions of the Great Accord.

Gulaya: a star-shaped charm, usually made of metal, that is anchored to a specific location and can take its wearer back there at need. They are rare, and difficult to recharge.

Hawk Hill: near Solantha, on the other side of Firegate Bridge; the location of the mages' hidden Temple.

Hedgewitch: a variety of mage specialized in earth-based magic.

Herald, The: the main newspaper in Solantha, catering mostly to the majority human population. It used to belong to the media conglomerate of Thorgana Mills, the Benefactor, and while in new hands, is still not particularly mage-friendly.

Iannis: see ar'Sannin, Iannis.

Janta Urama: mage and scholar, head librarian in the Solantha Mages Guild, and foster mother of Tinari Schaun, a young girl whose human family rejected her for having magic.

Kelling, Barrla: Mina's best friend from rural Abbsville, who worked in her parents' general store and loves shifter romances. She came to Solantha with Fenris, Mina and her boyfriend Marris Dolan, to help uncover the Resistance plot there.

Lady, The: mages refer to the First Mage, Resinah, as the Lady, most often in the phrase "by the Lady!"

Liu: a young Garaian girl Sunaya and Iannis brought back from their travels, who is training to be a chef under Mrs. Tandry in the palace kitchens, and wants to open her own restaurant eventually.

Loranian: the difficult, secret language of magic that all mages are required to master.

Lowry, Gardina: an exclusive Solantha dressmaker patronized by Sunaya.

Mages Guild: the governmental organization that rules the mages in each state, and supervises the other races. The headquarters are usually in the same building as the Palace of the local Chief Mage, to whom the Guild is subordinate.

Magitech: devices that are powered by both magic and technology.

Magorah: the god of the shifters, associated with the moon.

Manuc: an island country off the west coast of the Central Continent, where Chief Mage Iannis ar'Sannin was born and educated. It is also the country where the legendary Tua most often interact with humans.

Manucan: the language of Manuc, an island country northwest of the Central Continent.

Marris: see Dolan, Marris.

Marwale: a luxurious hotel on the west coast, about an hour from Solantha, the capital of Canalo. It caters to mages and rich humans.

Melcott, Annia: a human enforcer and close friend of Sunaya. After Annia's younger sister Noria was sentenced to hard labor in the Mines and disappeared during the great earthquake, Annia set off to find her sibling and has not yet returned.

Melcott, Noria: Annia Melcott's younger sister, a gifted inventor who used to work part-time in the shop Over the Hedge, belonging to Comenius Genhard. She had a mage boyfriend, Elnos Ragga, but left him to join the Resistance, and was subsequently sentenced to hard labor in the mines. However, during the great quake she disappeared and has not yet resurfaced.

Mills, Thorgana: socialite and former owner of a news media conglomerate as well as numerous other companies. After being exposed as the Benefactor, the financier and mastermind behind the Resistance, she was imprisoned. She managed to escape during a prison fire, but later died around the time of the Solantha earthquake.

Mina: a young mage engaged to Sunaya's friend Fenris. Mina's original name is Tamina Marton, and from childhood she was called "Mina" by her friends and family. After running away as a teenager, she used the name Mina Hollin and eventually, various other pseudonyms as needed.

Mindspeak: shifters' telepathic way to communicate over short distances, especially useful when in animal form. A few mages also share this ability.

Minister, the: the mage who presides the Convention of Chief

Mages, and coordinates the affairs of the Northia Federation between sessions, particularly foreign relations. The office is currently held by Zavian Graning.

Moredo, Maltar: chief shareholder and CEO of **Moredo Constructions**, currently the largest construction company in Solantha.

Nebara: one of the fifty states making up the Northia Federation, located north of Canalo, and Fenris's home state.

Nelia: see under Thrase, Nelia.

Noria: see under Melcott, Noria.

Northia Federation: a federation consisting of fifty states that cover almost the entire northern half and middle of the Western Continent. The Federal Government is located in the capital Dara, on the east coast.

Northian: the main language spoken in the Northia Federation.

Over the Hedge: a shop at Witches' End selling magical charms and herbal remedies, belonging to Comenius Genhard.

Pernia: a country on the Central Continent, from which Sunaya's friend Comenius Genhard hails.

Polar: see under ar'Tollis, Polar.

Ragga, Elnos: mage and inventor, formerly Noria Melcott's boyfriend. He and Noria worked together to develop new magitech devices. Since she left, he has been collaborating with Chief Mage Iannis on various projects, and advises him on scientific and technical issues.

Recca: the world of humans, mages and shifters.

Resinah: the first mage, whose teachings are of paramount spiritual importance for the mages. Her statue can be found in the mage temples, which are off-limits to non-mages and magically hidden from outsiders.

Resistance: a movement of revolutionaries planning to overthrow the mages and take control of the Northia Federation. Over time they became bolder and more aggressive, using terrorist attacks with civilian casualties, as well as assassinations. The discovery that their main financier, the so-called Benefactor and the other human leaders of the Resistance were planning to turn on their shifter allies dealt a blow to the unity of the movement. While the Resistance appears defanged for the moment, its human adherents are still hoping for a resurgence.

Rusalia, see under Genhard, Rusalia.

Rylan: see under Baine, Rylan.

ar'Sannin, Iannis: Chief Mage of Canalo; Sunaya's master and fiancé. He resides in the capital city of Solantha, from which he runs Canalo as well as the Mages Guild with the help of his deputy, Director Chen, and various Secretaries. Originally a native of Manuc, a country located across the Eastern Sea. His impending wedding to his apprentice, the half-shifter Sunaya Baine, has drawn world-wide media attention.

Secretary: in each state, the Chief Mages are assisted by Secretaries (Finance, Reconstruction, Legal, Agriculture, etc.), some of whom may eventually achieve the rank of Chief Mage themselves.

Serapha charms: paired amulets that allow two people, usually a couple, to find each other via twinned stones imbued with a small part of their essence. Normally, only the wearer can take a serapha charm off.

Shifter: a human who can change into animal form and back by magic. They originally resulted from illegal experiments by mages on ordinary humans.

Shiftertown: the part of Solantha where the official shifter clans live.

Skonel, Wellmore: human; since the retirement of his predecessor, Captain of Solantha's Enforcers. He does not relish having to work with Sunaya in reforming the Enforcer's Guild.

Slade, Rubb: a sleazy journalist covering the Convention and wedding.

Solantha: the capital of Canalo State, a port city on the west coast of the Northia continent. Seat of Chief Mage Iannis ar'Sannin and the Canalo Mages Guild, and home of Sunaya Baine.

Solantha Bay: spanned by the Firegate Bridge, the bay gave its name to the city and port that became the capital of Canalo.

Solantha Palace: the seat of power in Canalo, where both the Chief Mage and the Mages Guild reside. It is located near the coast of Solantha Bay.

Solantha Press Club: an institution dedicated to supporting the press, known for its well-stocked bar.

Southia: the subcontinent to the south of Northia, composed of various nations. Northia and Southia together form the Western Continent.

Sunaya: see under Baine, Sunaya.

Mrs. Tandry: human, head chef in the kitchens of Solantha Palace, who supervises Liu's apprenticeship there.

Testing: human and shifter schoolchildren in the Northia Federation are tested for magic at least twice during their schoolyears, and a positive result used to lead to the magic wipe (often with permanent mental damage). Sunaya, who has a personal stake in the subject as a potential victim of this process, is now in charge of Testing in Canalo, and tries to find more humane solutions on a case-to-case basis.

Thorgana: see under Mills, Thorgana.

Thrase, Nelia: a young human, Sunaya's social secretary, who used to be a journalist before her current job.

Tinari Schaun: a young human girl who tested positive for magic, and was rejected by her human parents. She has been informally adopted by mage librarian Janta Urama.

ar'Tollis, Polar: former Chief Mage of Nebara, who was condemned to death in absentia for a crime against the Great Accord – namely, to save the life of a child with illegal magic, who had attacked a mage. He disappeared just before he was to be arrested, and despite a nation-wide manhunt, has never resurfaced.

Toring, Garrett: mage, Federal Director of Security, former

Federal Secretary of Justice. An ambitious high official in the Federal government, determined to expand his power, and catch the fugitive former Chief Mage Polar ar'Tollis.

Trouble: a non-corporeal ether parrot that resulted when Sunaya tried the ether pigeon spell on her own. He appears whenever Sunaya pronounces his name in any context.

Tua: a legendary and highly dangerous race of very long-lived beings with powerful magic, who sometimes cross from their own world into Recca, most frequently in Manuc.

Ur-God: the name the humans call the Creator by.

Vanderheim, Curian: human millionaire and businessman, husband to the late Thorgana Mills. After his wife's arrest, he managed to flee the country with some of his vast fortune.

Watawis: one of the fifty states of the Northia Federation, land-locked, in the mountainous northwest. It is one of the least populated and poorest of the fifty states.

Witches' End: a pier in Solantha City, part of the Port, where immigrant magic users sell their wares and services.

Words: Loranian formulas used by mages for almost all standard spells.

Zavian Graning: see under Graning, Zavian.

ABOUT THE AUTHOR

JASMINE WALT is obsessed with books, chocolate, and sharp objects. Somehow, those three things melded together in her head and transformed into a desire to write, usually fantastical stuff with a healthy dose of action and romance. Her characters are a little (okay, a lot) on the snarky side, and they swear, but they mean well. Even the villains sometimes.

When Jasmine isn't chained to her keyboard, you can find her practicing her triangle choke on the jujitsu mat, spending time with her family, or binge-watching superhero shows on Netflix.

Want to connect with Jasmine? You can find her on Instagram at @jasmine.walt, on Facebook, or at www.jasminewalt.com.

ALSO BY JASMINE WALT

The Dragon's Gift Trilogy

Coauthored with May Sage

Dragon's Gift

Dragon's Blood—Coming Soon!

Dragon's Legacy—Coming Soon!

The Baine Chronicles: Fenris's Story:

Forsaken by Magic (Novella)

Fugitive by Magic

Claimed by Magic

Saved by Magic

The Baine Chronicles Series:

Burned by Magic

Bound by Magic

Hunted by Magic

Marked by Magic

Betrayed by Magic

Deceived by Magic

Scorched by Magic

Taken by Magic

Tested by Magic (novella)

The Nia Rivers Adventures:

Coauthored with Ines Johnson

Dragon Bones

Demeter's Tablet

Templar Scrolls

Serpent Mound—Coming Soon!

Eden's Garden—Coming Soon!

The Gatekeeper Chronicles:

Coauthored with Debbie Cassidy

Marked by Sin

Hunted by Sin

Claimed by Sin

Made in the USA
Columbia, SC
16 July 2019